Breeze
on a
Journey

Rebecca McCartney

WESTBOW
PRESS®
A DIVISION OF THOMAS NELSON
& ZONDERVAN

WestBow Press books may be ordered through booksellers or by contacting:

WestBow Press
A Division of Thomas Nelson & Zondervan
1663 Liberty Drive
Bloomington, IN 47403
www.westbowpress.com
844-714-3454

ISBN: 978-1-6642-3978-4 (sc)
ISBN: 978-1-6642-3977-7 (e)

Print information available on the last page.

WestBow Press rev. date: 7/28/2021

To Cynthia, without whose love and encouragement
this book never would have happened.

Prologue

SHE WASN'T SURE how long she fell but she knew when she hit the bottom. She lay still, paralyzed by the intensity of the pain permeating through her body and into her soul. The cold, stone floor gave nothing on impact. Her body absorbed it all. The pain slicing through her head eradicated rational thought. She blinked, but her pupils did not dilate. The blackness around her was so complete, she could not tell where it ended and she began. There was no boundary between her and it.

A moan escaped her lips but she knew she was speaking only to herself in the dark abyss of this pit when she murmured, "I hurt."

"Yes, it will do that to you."

If she had the ability, she would have been startled but as it was she could only lie still and wonder who else could possibly be down here in the deepest hole she could ever imagine. Her eyes searched uselessly in the dark for the sound of the voice. Suddenly, she saw him.

A man, dressed in linen pants, a loose green shirt with rolled-up sleeves and a brown leather vest was perched comfortably on a rock a few feet away with one leg drawn up and his arm resting on his knee. She wondered how she could see him in this intense darkness. There was no light shining from above or from his face like how she imagined an angel would be. She could simply see him. He had long steel gray hair streaked with silver which was pulled back by a leather strap at his neck. He was lean, but his sinewy forearms and calloused hands showed that he did not lack strength. Deep lines were etched around his mouth and eyes, maybe from worry or laughing or both. Beneath his strongly pronounced nose, his lips turned up softly at the corners. A keen sharpness to his eyes made her look away for fear he would know her whole story with just a moment's gaze.

"What will do that to you?" she asked, coming to herself and remembering his comment.

"The truth."

"What about the truth?"

"It will do that to you."

Either he was being deliberately cryptic or the fall had addled her brain.

"Will do what to you?" she asked, an edge of annoyance creeping into her voice.

"It will hurt you."

There was something about the knowing sound of his voice or maybe it was the unexpected gentleness in his response, but it cracked her. Like an egg that shatters from the slightest tap, all the pain came spilling out of her; the exhaustion, the confusion…the betrayal. She was embarrassed to be crying in front of this stranger, but it wasn't a choice anymore. Her body convulsed with sobs so powerful they threatened to crack a rib. At times she screamed her pain, a raw primal sound that magnified itself on the cave walls. Other times her mouth was fixed silently open in a scream only angels could hear.

Sometime during her sobbing, the man had moved closer to her. Common sense told her she should be alarmed but something deeper, something she couldn't explain, told her there was nothing to fear. When the last drop of sorrow was finally trickling out, she lay silent and exhausted. There was a stillness inside she hadn't felt in a long time. Her face was wet and slightly swollen. Small shudders shook her body at infrequent intervals.

He reached out a hand to help her up and she took it. A healing warmth immediately flowed into her body. It didn't completely eradicate the pain but it lessened it so that she could move freely again. Startled, she looked at him, questioning him with her eyes. Amused, he returned her gaze but his steady look gave nothing away.

"Who are you?" she asked softly.

"I am an old man," he responded.

"Should I call you that then? Old Man?" Breeze raised one eyebrow, a glimmer of a smile appearing on her face.

"If you like," he replied, pulling a neatly folded handkerchief out of his leather vest and handing it to her.

At first, she was afraid to touch it. It was the whitest thing she had ever seen and she was so dirty from her dash through the woods and encounter with the cave floor. But the snot and tears were drying on her face, making it stiff and uncomfortable, so she took it. The fabric had an unworldly softness, like it had come from the robe of some heavenly being. Slowly, she unfolded it and pressed it to her face with both hands just to soak in the ethereal softness of it. Once again, healing power flowed into her, smoothing the lines in her forehead and soothing her thoughts.

"What is your name?" The Old Man's voice interrupted her moment with the handkerchief.

She refused to move the fabric from her face so her reply was somewhat muffled.

"Breeze."

"Breeze? Really? Is that your real name?"

She had the vague sense he already knew the answer to that question but answered anyway.

"No."

"What is your real name?"

"I'll tell you that when you tell me yours, Old Man."

To her surprise, he chuckled.

"Fair enough," he conceded. "Why do they call you Breeze?"

"Because my Dad always says I am as pleasant as a summer breeze," she explained.

"Well, Breeze, do you know why you're here?"

What did he mean by that, she thought, immediately irritated. *I'm here because I was running blindly through the forest and fell through a hole.*

As if he sensed her thoughts he responded, "You're here because you can't fix the mess you're in."

She felt tears begin to well in her eyes again but she pushed them back down. The otherworldliness of the Old Man was no longer surprising her, so she didn't question how he knew anything about "the mess" she was in.

"The only thing you can fix," he continued, "is yourself."

"Me?!" Anger flared like fire in her chest. "I'm not the one who needs fixing! If it weren't for that lying, selfish, unfaithful beast of a knight, I wouldn't be here in the first place!"

"Whoa, Breeze," the Old Man chuckled. "Or should I call you Tempest?"

She shot him a scorching look until he took her hand in his own. There it was again. What was that? She felt the anger drain from her body through her hand, as if he were taking it from her. In its place she felt peace and reassurance.

"It's time for you to go home," he said.

Chapter One

$\mathcal{B}$REEZE WAS IN her happy place. Flowers, herbs, vegetables, and berries were bursting to life in the garden behind her family's apothecary shop. Each had a purpose; some were for nourishment, others for healing. Even some of the weeds, like the broad-leafed plantains and the spunky little dandelions, were harvested for their healing properties.

The plants were in their showing off season. Bee balm and dill were explosions of pink and yellow, like rambunctious toddlers calling, "Look, look!" to their mother Earth. The serene golden heads of the fever few with crowns of white petals swayed in the breeze, while the proud lavender stood as sentinels over their healing army.

With the noon-day sun warming her back Breeze absently wove the stems of daisies into a chain to hang in her hair. She was supposed to be gathering the daisies to make a salve for the poor farmer a few miles out of town who had been kicked by an ornery cow during milking. Normally a conscientious worker who took great pride in assisting her father with his work, Breeze was too distracted by more exciting things this morning than an old farmer and his smelly cow.

News had trickled into the shop like honey from a beehive that Drake McArthur was back in town. Breeze had been in love with Lord Hadrian's nephew ever since the young orphan had first come into his uncle's charge at just nine years of age. Every chance she could, she would drag her friend Caroline to the knights' practice fields where Drake would be predictably perched on a fence, staring straight ahead, saying nothing to anyone. Crouching just out of sight, the love-struck six-year old would invent stories, much to her friend's delight, in which she was always the distressed maiden and Drake the handsome knight who saved her over and over in a thousand different, but always valiant ways. Despite her endless hours of daydreaming, when the talented, aspiring knight left three years ago to further his training, he still couldn't remember her name, but Breeze knew there was a chance that could all change now.

She had shot up like a young sapling during Drake's absence and she knew from the reactions of the men that came into her father's shop that she was in the full bloom of womanhood. *Let's see if he doesn't remember my name now,* she thought, inwardly glowing at the imagined thought of their first meeting in three years, a meeting she had experienced so many times in her mind she knew exactly how it would go. She could perfectly picture how she would be in her best yellow dress, her trim waist beautifully accentuated by a sapphire blue ribbon. Her glossy brown hair would be swept up in mounds of gorgeously plaited braids with one tendril hanging down to frame her blushing cheek. His emerald eyes would be glowing with unabashed love and admiration. With one arm he would encircle her waist and with the other…

"Come help me with this plant."

Her father's voice snatched her out of Drake's imaginary arms and back onto the ground where she was kneeling. A real blush came to her cheek, but this time, it blossomed in the soil of embarrassment and not from the tender root of young love. Scrambling up to her feet, she hurried over.

Galen was bent low over the browning leaves of an orange marigold plant which was clearly in the later stages of root rot. Her father's dark brown hair, which sprouted from his head in wild disarray, was streaked with gold highlights as if the sun had reached down and tousled the hair

2

of a favorite child. His almond shaped green eyes were a perfect reflection of his beloved plants.

"With all the flowers in this garden, wouldn't it make more sense to pull this one up and throw it in with the chickens?"

Galen rubbed the brown stubble on his chin as he contemplated his floral patient.

"No, there is still life in this plant. It just needs some safety so it can heal."

Breeze looked dubiously at her father and then back at the plant. She had always felt he fell a little too heavily on the optimistic side, even with plants.

Looking around at the low spot in the garden which was prone to sogginess, she responded, "Seems to me that a plant who doesn't have the good sense to grow in a better spot isn't worth rescuing."

"Just you wait," Galen replied to Breeze's suspicious look, straightening his spine with a groan, "with a little time and love this plant is going to be healing wounds and lessening pain, just like it was meant to do. First though, we need to get it out of the mud and bring it inside."

Noticing her father's discomfort as he placed a hand on his dirty knee and slowly pushed himself up, she quickly grabbed a nearby pot and began scooping in handfuls of dirt from the compost pile.

"I can do it," she volunteered, kneeling in the sodden grass beside the plant.

"Thank you," her father said gratefully, gathering up the daisies Breeze had left on the ground. "I will get started on this salve. Remember to wash all the dirt off the roots and pull off all the diseased parts or the plant will still die, even after we get it out of the mud."

Already lost in her task, Breeze just nodded her head.

Her mother, Darla, appeared in the doorway, standing tall and straight, a stern expression on her face. Her black hair, tinged with gray, was pulled back tightly into a plaited bun. Her hands were clasped over a perfectly white apron which was fitted over a steel blue, no-nonsense dress. Not for the first time, Breeze was struck by how different her parents were. Her father was soft and nurturing, like the soil of his beloved garden. Her mother was more like the rocks of the garden wall that prevented the pigs and chickens from trampling the delicate plants.

"Aldwin is in the shop," she said simply, her gray-blue eyes glancing briefly at her daughter's disheveled appearance, and turned away.

"Dad, can I take care of Aldwin and get this plant later?" Breeze asked, trying to look nonchalant.

Her father gave her a knowing look and waved her off. "Go, go," he said, pretending to be annoyed. "I'll take care of the plant." The apothecary was all too aware of his daughter's obsession with Lord Hadrian's charge, though it caused him little concern. He knew it was as likely for the seasons to switch places as for someone of Drake's station to notice an apothecary's daughter.

Breeze tried not to run. As a friend of Aldwin, she would have been happy to see the castle guard under any circumstances due to the sunshine he seemed to carry in his smile on even the dreariest of days, but she also knew that if anyone would have information about Drake, it would be his childhood best friend. Her pulse quickened as she hastily wiped her muddy hands on her white apron. She knew her mother would have something to say about that but what could she do? It wasn't her fault harvesting healing from the Earth was a dirty job.

Right before entering the shop at the front of their house Breeze remembered her hair. She hadn't taken a moment to brush it this morning. It was all the sunshine's fault. It had snuck through her window and enticed her down the stairs and out into its warm embrace without taking a proper moment to make herself presentable to the world. She stood hesitating, glancing back and forth between the doorway to the shop and the stairs to her loft. After a moment she thought, "Oh, who cares? It's just Aldwin and I can't wait another breath for news of Drake!"

The moment she rounded the corner her breath stopped all together. Drake.

Her heart dropped like a stone. This is not the way she wanted it to be!

He had filled out since she had seen him three years ago but even from the back she would still recognize him anywhere. She stood staring at the wavy black hair tied at the nape of the neck, the broad muscular back clothed in a wine-red tunic angling down towards the trim waist encircled with a leather belt and ornamented with a fine sword and scabbard. His black breeches fit to perfection and his brown leather boots lacked even a single scuff.

Realizing Drake and Aldwin, who were chatting together near the doorway, still hadn't noticed her, she quietly placed one foot behind her and began to ease herself slowly out of the room. She felt a small bump at her elbow followed by the sounds of smashing glass and the strong scent of peppermint. Looking down at the amber colored bottle she had just knocked off the shelf, she knew her dreams of Drake falling instantly in love with her had just shattered on the floor.

They both turned to her then and she froze to the spot, feeling like a dirty, ugly troll. Drake glanced at her for a moment from the doorway where he was leaning, recognition dawning, and then turned his attention back to the passersby on the busy street. And that was it. No magic. No love at first sight. She was as inconsequential as she had ever been.

Breeze clenched her fists and her teeth. This was her dad's fault! She never left anything out of place in the shop. The workroom in the back reflected her father's messy brilliance but the shop front was her domain, with copper bowls and amber bottles lined neatly on the shelves like obedient children awaiting their commands. Each morning she filled a vase next to the door with whatever plants the season offered and hung only the best smelling herbs to dry above the counter. The joy she felt at serving customers was reflected in the loving care she took of her family's tiny shop front.

Aldwin was instantly at her feet, carefully gathering the glass into a handkerchief he pulled from his tunic pocket. The sight of Aldwin's blonde head bent over the smashed bottle brought her to her senses. She snatched a rag from a hook on the wall and knelt beside Aldwin's wiry frame. He flashed her a familiar smile, full of sunshine and warmth, but her heart was frozen with shame.

Over Aldwin's shoulder, Breeze saw the slight figure of Caroline, her dearest friend, appear in the doorway. Even though they were the same age, Caroline barely reached Breeze's chin. It was as if her body had gotten distracted in the process of growing and forgotten to finish the job. She was so petite she probably could have walked right under Drake's line of vision without him even noticing her. But he did notice her, and Breeze had never before so badly wanted to see and not see her friend at the same time.

Caroline was beautiful in an open, friendly sort of way and boys buzzed around her like the only dandelion in a field of green grass after a long, hard winter. She had hair the color of spring wheat and eyes the color of summer twilight. From her place on the floor, Breeze saw Drake's eyes linger on the sight of her lovely friend and heard his deep, resonant voice say, "Good morning, Caroline."

Resentment welled up in Breeze. Why did Caroline have to look so lovely today? She was a baker's daughter after all. Couldn't she have some flour on her shirt or jam on her nose? Since they were little girls Caroline was usually covered in flour and Breeze was covered in dirt. Why today of all days did she look so perfect?

Caroline had to tilt her head way back to look into Drake's face, but when she did she gifted him one of her radiant, infectious smiles. She wasn't being seductive, Breeze knew. It was just the way she smiled. Actually, it was just the way she lived, with her heart open to the world. A corner of Drake's mouth turned up slightly in response, and then he returned his gaze to the street. Caroline, unfazed by the minimal response, moved on into the shop.

It took a moment for her eyes to adjust to the light but she eventually spotted her friend, still kneeling on the floor.

"I was stopping by to let you know I will…" and then it all dawned on Caroline and her eyes wrote a book for Breeze's heart to read. Caroline noticed her friend's bedraggled appearance, the shattered bottle, and the aloof object of her friend's affections standing disinterestedly by the door. Their silent conversation about Breeze's shattered hopes lasted less than a second, but Breeze knew her friend understood.

"…be a little late for our walk this evening," Caroline finally finished out loud. "Dad has a special event at the castle he needs help preparing for."

Caroline and Breeze had gone on a walk every night their parents allowed it for as long as they both could remember. Theirs was a friendship that had literally formed in sunshine and in rain. And snow and sleet and every other version of weather their particular part of the country could invent. They loved it all. The biting winter nights with moonlight shattering into a million tiny pieces on the snow punctuated by the crunch of their boots were just as welcome as the warm summer evenings lit by fireflies and serenaded by frogs. Their nightly walks were how they put each day to bed, looking it over, cleaning it up and tucking it snugly into their memories.

"I'll come help as soon as I can," answered Breeze, rising with the oil-soaked rag and shattered glass in her hand.

"So, you will both be at Drake's coming home party," Aldwin chimed in brightly.

"Slavery party more like it," Drake mumbled darkly from the doorway, casting an awkward silence across the room.

Aldwin tried to smooth things over with a smile. "Well, ladies, I hope to see you both at the party."

"When have you ever seen us at these parties?" Breeze replied grumpily. "We stay in the kitchens."

Caroline's eyes widened at Breeze's rude comment. Then with a cheery tone, said to Breeze, "I'll see you in a bit then. The sky is looking like it will be a beautiful night for a walk when we're done with our work." Caroline gave Breeze a long meaningful we-can-talk-about-this-then look, and disappeared out the door.

With Caroline gone Breeze's embarrassment at her appearance returned like an illness, spreading blotchy red patches across her cheeks. Drawing on years of experience in assisting her father with life or death situations, she forced herself to stay calm.

"Aldwin, you are here for the stinging nettle for Lord Hadrian's arthritis, I presume?"

"That I am," responded Aldwin.

As quick as humanly possible Breeze fetched the nettle cream and handed it to the castle guard who began to open his money pouch.

"We'll add it to Lord Hadrian's account," Breeze said quickly. "You must be getting back to get ready for the party and I need to get back to the garden." Not hardly believing her own boldness but needing this experience to end, she took them both by the elbow and gave them what her dad might have called a shove out the door, but her dad was still in the back room so it didn't matter what he would have called it.

As soon as they were gone the unfortunate lover allowed her head to sink to the counter where she began banging it softly until the sound of laughter brought it snapping back up again. Boulder, the blacksmith's son, was standing right in front of her. Coal black coils of hair framed his broad face and copper rings encircled the pupils of his soft brown eyes. His name wasn't really Boulder but it was what everyone had called him for so long on account of his massive frame no one remembered his real name.

"Oh my," he said, laughing even harder when he saw her face and the front of her dress. "You look like you lost a fight with a mud puddle. And your hair! Did the sunshine drag you outside before your mirror got to say anything about it?"

Crossing her arms in front of her chest, Breeze scowled petulantly.

"I know at least a dozen different ways I could poison you, you know."

"Ah, but you wouldn't," he replied jovially, "Your father would never forgive you."

This was true. The blacksmith and the apothecary had been friends since childhood and had raised their children in almost constant companionship. Breeze distinctly remembers the day her father tried to explain to her that she was actually an only child and that Boulder was not her brother.

"Did you need something or were you just bored from driving off all your dad's customers?"

"Well, I thought I needed some of that special burn salve you make but as soon as I saw you I realized that all I really needed was to see you looking that way. It just made my whole day." Boulder's lips were pressed together in an effort to control his laughter but his chest shook like a small earthquake with the effort.

"I don't like you."

"Yes, you do," Boulder said, stepping around the counter to throw a bronze-skinned arm around Breeze. "You love me."

"No," she responded, pushing Boulder playfully away. "I love Drake McArthur."

"Yes, that's right," Boulder said knowingly, nodding his head. "Lord Perfection of the High Castle. Very good choice. Very good choice."

"Here's your salve," Breeze said, ignoring his sarcasm, "and would you like some wolf's bane for the pain? Although remember if he puts it in his mouth your father will be looking for a new apprentice."

"Best not to tempt him at this point," Boulder laughed.

Breeze recorded the sale in the ledger and closed the book. "Let me tell

Dad I'm leaving and then I'll walk with you. I need to go help Caroline make cakes for the castle party this evening."

With every step Breeze took toward the bakery a plan began to rise in her mind. So deep she was in thought, who knows how many unsuspecting travelers she might have collided with if it hadn't been for her hand resting on the inside of Boulder's arm. As he guided her down the street her resolve grew with every step. She was going to make this right. Drake was going to notice her tonight. And she knew how to make it happen.

Chapter Two

$\int$MELLS AND SOUNDS overwhelmed Breeze. After hours of hard work, she was finally carrying the tray that contained just a small portion of the mounds of food that she and Caroline had slaved over all while Breeze told in great detail how *this* time was going to be different; *this* time she was going to impress Drake McArthur. She wasn't yet sure how she was going to make it into the ballroom, but she knew she would find a way. She had to. Caroline listened patiently and promised to be waiting to hear all the news of her triumph on their evening walk.

With barely time to spare, Breeze had rushed home to get ready, brushing and braiding her hair into submission until it lay on her head in well-behaved, glossy, rose-scented piles. Her corset was cinched until she could barely breathe so that her already small waist looked even smaller. With a pair of scissors, she cut away at the lace neckline of her nicest dress which her mother had sewn almost to her chin. If she was going to get the attention of the handsome, young squire, she thought as she hastily hemmed the lower neck line, she wasn't going to do it looking like a nun.

Breeze arrived with Caroline's family, along with piles of date loafs, spiced pears, almond cakes, sweet breads and more. As soon as they began bringing food into the kitchen, Breeze noticed the frantic pace. Well-dressed servants and frazzled looking kitchen maids rushed around each other while the head cook barked orders above the din. Instead of setting down the platter she was carrying, as Caroline had done, Breeze rushed up to the head cook and offered to take the tray into the ballroom herself. Cook briefly glanced at her, noticed her well-groomed appearance, and gave a curt nod. Breeze forced herself to put a lid on the celebration that wanted to burst out of her.

In the ballroom, hundreds of flames joined the festivities by dancing on their wicks, casting their lights onto the rough stone walls. Thick gray columns of stone soared high while heavy blue drapery hung low. She thought of her friend Anna, a castle servant, who she knew had spent the entire day scrubbing the smooth stone floors, just to have them soiled again by hundreds of feet.

The crowd jostled her as she clung almost desperately to the platter. Music, talking, laughter and all the other sounds a hundred nobles make when crammed into a single room pressed on her ears. There was such a press of bodies around the edge of the room, she felt stuck. With each moment the precariously balanced platter of food teetered dangerously between landing on the floor and decorating her dress, as she inched her way toward the food table. Desperately, she wondered how she would ever find Drake in such a crowd.

Resentment began to well-up in Breeze. The town of Northwell was a small one as was its castle. Even though this was not her social circle, she knew many of these people as everyone from the richest lord to the poorest widow grew ill and needed an apothecary's care. Why couldn't they give her a little room? Why were they not even looking at her?

She glanced around at those closest to her. There was young Lord Guthrie, tall, slender and good-looking, smiling too brightly and laughing too loudly, as he worked to gain the attention of a beautiful young lady draped in silks and adorned with jewels. Breeze had half a mind to tell the young woman about the poultices she used to make for the warts on Guthrie's fingers when they were both children. It was one of the first medicines her father had taught her to make. To her other side she saw Lord Chaldrin. She remembered the afternoon she spent holding the hand of his good arm as her father worked to set a broken bone on the other after the aging Lord had been thrown from his spirited horse.

In front of her, like a wall of opulent drapery, was Lady Collins, simpering and giggling, with a rope of pearls around her neck and fountains of lace pouring down the front of her bodice. Breeze remembered her differently. She remembered Lady Collins with disheveled hair framing a face swollen from crying, with pale blue bags under red-rimmed eyes as she held her sick infant. Breeze remembered how the baby boy lay limp, struggling for every breath.

There had been an outbreak of the dreaded croup and her father was left frantically rushing from house to house. So, he had left his daughter, just on the cusp of becoming a young woman, with a set of careful instructions and a heartfelt prayer. By the morning, Breeze was exhausted, but the baby was sleeping peacefully, evenly pulling life-giving air into his lungs. The grateful mother had wept and clung to Breeze, thanking her over and over again.

The little boy was four now and apparently all was forgotten Breeze thought irritably as Lady Collins bumped, yet again, into the heavy, unbalanced platter. Breeze had half a mind to just dump it on Lady Collins and storm out. Why had she thought this would work?

And then he was there, like the stories she had made up in her head a thousand times, rescuing her. With one arm he lifted the heavy platter and with the other he encircled her waist. The crowd parted for him and they passed through easily. This was partly because he was a head taller than Breeze, partly because of his status as Lord Hadrian's nephew, and partly because Drake was the kind of person whose presence demanded your attention.

After depositing the desserts on a table already laden with food, he turned to her and bowed deeply. When he lifted his forest green eyes to hers, Breeze felt a surge of triumph. She *knew* that look. He wasn't just looking at her, he was *looking* at her. Without a word, he lifted her hand and escorted her to the dance floor.

And they danced, again and again they danced. She should have felt tired. She should have remembered Caroline was waiting for her. But all she felt was heaven. As she and Drake twirled and skipped and danced her feet felt only the rhythm of the music. Her body released its joy with every twist and turn. Each time they turned around and his smile landed back on her it was like magic. Each time his large, calloused hand pressed against hers she felt it all the way to her toes.

All at once, instead of pressing his hand to hers in the dance, he grabbed her by the wrist, pulling her to the side and towards a doorway exiting the room.

"Come," he said. "This way."

Breeze glanced around, trying to discern what had caused the sudden change. Her eyes landed briefly on the confused face of Elaine.

Elaine. Perfect hair. Perfect face. Perfect figure. She even had as close as one could come to a perfect personality. Despite being set to inherit a large dowry as the daughter of one of the wealthiest lords around, she was authentically kind to everyone.

But then like a sorcerer's illusion, Elaine was gone and they were rushing away from the noise and the dancing down a dark, stone hallway

"Where are we going?" she asked.

"I forgot to feed Balius," he responded.

"The horse? We're going to feed your horse?"

"He's not mine. He's my uncle's, but yes, we are going to feed him. A knight's horse is one of his greatest assets and must not be neglected."

Drake pulled her through the final doorway into the night. The soothing night air washed over her, instantly relaxing her body. The loud clamor of the ballroom was replaced by the quiet chirping of crickets. The stars were out in full force with an ocean of lights that poured itself all the way to the horizon.

She became aware that Drake was still holding her hand as he led her toward the stables. As they were about to enter the stable door Breeze stopped.

"I'm not sure I should go in," she said, hesitating.

Knight's horses were enormous and notoriously feisty. The last thing she needed right now was a serious injury from a startled war horse.

Drake slipped his arm around her waist and smiled down at her.

"It will be fine," he coaxed, "Balius is just a big baby. He comes alive in the jousting ring, but in his stall he's a gentle lamb. Trust me."

He said the last two words with a mischievous tilt to his smile and a dance in his eyes that suggested she shouldn't, but with his strong arm still around her waist and his face close to hers, she couldn't bring herself to walk away. In all her childhood daydreaming, could she have ever imagined a moment like this? She had to savor every second.

"I'll try," she acquiesced.

"Come on. You'll love him," Drake promised.

The only light in the stable came from the stars shining their light through the open stall windows. Breeze heard whinnying, snorting, and the stomping of hooves as they walked across the dirt floor. At the end of the row she could see the silhouette of a colossal black horse munching contentedly from a hay-filled trough.

"Is that Balius?" Breeze asked.

"It is," replied Drake, beaming with obvious pride.

Breeze lifted an eyebrow. "I thought you said you forgot to feed him."

"Oh. Uh…his apples. I forgot to feed him his apples. It's his favorite."

Drake walked over to a half-size barrel full of apples and grabbed a few. He held one out to Breeze, "Would you like to feed him?"

Breeze took the offered apple uncertainly. Her head was barely level with the horse's muscular chest. His face and mouth were easily twice the size of Ginger, her father's swift-footed travelling horse back home.

"My fingers are actually an extremely valuable part of my work as an apothecary. My father would not be pleased if I came home without them."

Drake laughed. She wasn't sure why but the sound was like an elixir. She loved the deepness of it and the way it came out like clear water from a spring. A warm glow swelled inside her to know she had inspired his laughter.

"I'll help you." Drake stood behind Breeze so closely she could feel his chest against her back and the side of his chin pressed lightly against her forehead. He reached his hand under hers and used his thumb to pull her fingers flat. With his other hand he placed the apple in the center of her palm and pushed it toward Balius. Realizing he was getting a treat, Balius lifted his head from his dinner of hay and pointed his ears forward. Then he brought his huge mouth down toward the apple. Breeze pressed her body back against Drake and squeezed her eyes shut. She felt the soft tickle of horse lips as Balius carefully took the proffered treat. This time she was the one who laughed as she opened her eyes.

"You really are just a big baby, aren't you?" she said, reaching up to stroke the horse's soft neck and give him a little scratch under his mane.

"Would you like to ride him?" Drake asked.

"What? Won't we get in trouble?"

"Maybe," Drake admitted, "But we might also enjoy a scenic ride through the trees under a starry night sky on a big, gentle, baby of a horse. Seems worth the risk to me."

Again, Breeze knew she should say no. She wasn't one to break the rules and she wasn't going to let herself even think what her father might think of the idea. But, again, she couldn't bring herself to leave, to walk away from the opportunity to be close to him just a little longer. She wanted to live out this waking dream until life forced her to wake up.

When she turned to look up at him their faces were just a breath apart.

"Let's take a risk," she whispered.

A slow smile broke across his face. He walked around, opened Balius' stall, and made a clicking sound. Balius walked out of his stall and stood still.

"Do you need to put anything on him?" Breeze asked.

"No, Balius and I have known each other for a long time. We get along just fine without all the extras."

With a leap that showcased his athleticism, Drake leapt onto the horse's back.

"Wait, Drake," Breeze hesitated, "I…I forgot I was in a dress."

"No fear, my lady. We will have you ride sideways so as to protect your modesty. Hold up your hand."

Reaching down, Drake locked arms with Breeze and pulled her easily up in front of him, wrapping his arms around her waist to grab onto Balius' mane.

With a slight squeeze of Drake's legs, they headed slowly out into the night. Within minutes they reached the edge of the forest and disappeared into the trees. Leaves rustling in the wind combined with the steady sway of Balius' broad back to relax Breeze. She leaned back and lay her head against Drake's neck. She wondered how this moment could be any more perfect. Then Elaine's face came floating back into her mind.

"Were you running away from Elaine at the banquet?"

Balius' hooves continued their steady rhythm on the forest floor. Breeze could hear Drake's even breathing. For a moment there was no response and she wondered if he had heard her.

"Yes."

"Why?"

"I suppose you know that Uncle wants me to marry Elaine."

"I did know that," Breeze admitted quietly, feeling foolish, unfaithful even, though she knew that Drake and Elaine were not officially betrothed.

Why would someone as handsome as Drake want to be with someone like her when he could have Elaine?

Breeze's voice was barely above a whisper. "Seems like there are worse ways to spend your life than being married to someone as perfect as Elaine."

"No doubt she is wonderful," Drake agreed.

A painful stab of jealousy pierced Breeze's stomach and she sat up to put space between their bodies.

"I'm just not sure how I feel about being sold off as a marriage prospect because of my family name. If you were a slave, would you care if your master was beautiful?" Drake reasoned

"But Elaine is kind," Breeze countered, "I hardly think she would treat you as a slave."

"No, but it wouldn't change the truth that it was her providing for me and not the other way around."

They were both silent for a while, taking in the soothing sights and sounds of the forest at night.

Drake continued, "I would like to earn my own fortune and then marry whom I choose. It's not easy, but it is possible. If I win enough tournaments and get enough recognition, I could be offered my own land or even a castle, by the king. Would that not be better than to be married off to a wealthy merchant's daughter because my family had too many sons for too many generations to leave anything to me other than the great name of MacArthur?"

Breeze was surprised to hear an edge of bitterness creep into his voice. She decided not to think about Elaine right now. The night was beautiful, Drake was warm and strong and Balius was the most peaceful war horse she had ever had the privilege to sit astride. She leaned back into Drake again and rested her head against his neck. Her body felt pleasantly tired from the long day's work.

"Thank you for coming to my rescue tonight," she said.

"I was repaying a debt," he replied.

"What?" Breeze asked, shifting around to look in his face.

"What?" Drake feigned surprise. "You don't remember saving my young heart from despair?"

"I think I would remember such a heroic act," she laughed.

"But it's true," he insisted. "When I was about twelve years old, my dog, Baron, was sick. My uncle refused to try to help him, saying we should just cut off his head and end his misery, but I found Baron as a puppy shortly after moving here and…" Drake went quiet, struggling to control his emotions. "I just couldn't. I went to your dad on my own but he was too busy helping humans to help a young boy with his dog." He smiled wryly. "You overheard and offered to help. You were only nine at the time so I was skeptical but also, desperate. I agreed to let you look at Baron. You came with your little bag of medicines and some meat you snuck from your mom's kitchen. After looking over Baron, you grabbed some pouches and vials from your bag and made a ball of medicine with the meat. Somehow you convinced Baron to swallow the meat. I was worried you were just going to kill him faster but by that evening he was starting to come back to life. You came every day for a week and by the end Baron was healed… and I've been watching you ever since."

"How can you say that? I distinctly remember that experience and you never said one word to me, not during or after. You would stand like a stone against the wall while I was helping Baron and then afterwards you went back to acting like I didn't exist!" An awkward laugh escaped Breeze. She was trying not to show how painful the experience had been for her young heart.

"What can I say?" Drake shrugged his shoulders, "Showing emotion is not allowed in Lord Hadrian's household."

Both riders fell silent, lost in thought, as the dirt passed beneath their feet and the stars passed over their heads.

She heard the sound of cobblestones under Balius' hooves and was confused. She looked up and saw the apothecary shop. With a start she realized that she had fallen asleep. She sat up and looked around trying to get back into reality.

"Oh no, Drake, I am so sorry."

"I've been accused of being many things, but until tonight, boring was never one of them."

"No, no, it wasn't boring it was…It was perfect. Thank you." The last two words were almost a whisper.

It struck Breeze that here she was riding with Drake, late at night, on a war horse at the very center of town. Who knew who might be peeking through their window right now, it might even be her parents.

She leapt nimbly down from Balius and turned to give him a quick pat on the neck. "Thank you, Balius, for a wonderful evening," she said with a playful smile. Then she turned to dart into the shop.

"Wait!"

"Shhh! Drake," Breeze whispered fiercely, "do you want to be the center of town gossip from now until next harvest?"

"It wouldn't be the first time," he laughed, but thank the stars he laughed quietly. Then in a more serious tone, "Can we do this again?"

Breeze's heart was screaming at her to say yes but she simply smiled a coy smile, opened the shop door and disappeared inside.

Chapter Three

REEZE AWOKE THE next morning like one awakes from a pleasant dream. She could tell from the sunlight streaming through the window that it was later than she normally woke up, but still, she lay contentedly in her bed basking in the warm glow of sunlight as she relived the moments from last night. Then a single word shattered her dream world like a glass ball on a stone floor.

"Caroline!"

She jumped out of bed and hurriedly dressed. Pulling on her boots, she almost leapt down the stairs and raced past her mother who was sitting at a small wooden table next to the fireplace.

"In a hurry?" Darla asked, gazing down at papers in front of her. In an odd twist of the norm, her mother was the one who tracked all the finances of their family's apothecary. She said her husband was too soft-hearted. "He would be saving the world while we starved," she would complain.

"Yes, I need to go see Caroline."

"Hmmm," she muttered, still looking down. "Why?"

Trapped. Breeze hated dishonesty. She was always honest with her parents. They were calm, kind, reasonable people and Breeze had nothing to hide so there was no reason to lie to them. But she wasn't ready to share her experience with Drake yet. She still felt the glow of their beautiful evening together and she was fairly sure she could guess what her parents thought of Drake. Their reactions would ruin her moment.

"I left something at her house when we were preparing for the party at the castle."

Immediately, she felt sick. She hated the way lying to her mom made her feel, but now that she said it, she couldn't bear to tell her mom she had done it. When her mom looked up, Breeze saw something in her eyes but she wasn't sure what it was. Hurt, maybe? Or maybe that was Breeze's guilty conscience talking. It was time to leave this uncomfortable situation behind.

"I'll be back in a moment," she called out as she rushed into the shop and headed for the door. She almost ran right into Boulder who had appeared between her and the door.

"Uh, Boulder. Good day to you." Normally Breeze would have promptly set to work helping Boulder but today she looked frantically around figuring out how to escape. She stuck her head back in the other room. "Mom, where's Dad?"

"He left this morning to go deliver a salve."

Breeze knew that was the end of that. Taking care of customers in the shop was a job shared by her and her father. No problem. She could get this done quickly.

"Boulder, I have to go meet Caroline. Can we do this quickly?"

A knowing look came over Boulder's face. "No, I'll go. We can do it later." He turned toward the door, suspiciously eager to escape, but Breeze seized his arm.

"What do you know?" Breeze asked, lowering her eyebrows.

"Haven't you been telling me since we were kids that I know nothing," he evaded, staring at an indistinct point over Breeze's shoulder. Breeze gave up. Boulder could be as stubborn as his name suggested.

Dodging carts and people, Breeze darted across the street and raced the few shops down to Caroline's. As she stepped inside the bakery her nose was immediately transported to heaven, as it always was in the baker's shop. It wasn't that all the herbal remedies in her father's shop smelled bad. Some were pleasant and calming, but other remedies her dad cooked up seemed worse than the illness.

A loud thumping led Breeze to the back room where she found Caroline murdering a lump of dough. Caroline, whose hands were covered in white flour, was slamming the dough so hard onto the wooden table and then pounding it so vigorously with her fist Breeze considered backing quietly out of the door. She took her first tentative step backwards and then paused. Caroline meant more to her than that. This was worth repairing.

She cleared her throat. Caroline paused in her culinary homicide and looked up.

"Good day, Caroline," Breeze ventured with a weak smile.

Nothing. Thump. Thump. Thump. Slam! Thump. Thump. Thump. Slam!

"Caroline, I'm sorry."

Thump. Thump. Thump. Slam!

"Caroline, please," Breeze tried again. "You know how long I've loved Drake, ever since we were children!"

Thump. Thump. Thump. Slam!

"Caroline," an edge of irritation was creeping into Breeze's voice, "you would have done the same thing, you know you would."

Thump.

Caroline finally lifted her gaze. "No, actually, I don't know that I'm the kind of person who casts off a faithful friend for a nighttime rendezvous with someone to whom I mean nothing more than entertainment."

Caroline's unexpected blow bruised Breeze's heart.

"I came here hoping to share a wonderful moment with a dear friend but I can see you are too selfish to listen." And with that she stormed out of the shop.

At precisely that moment, two tears fell. One inside the shop, and one out of it.

Chapter Four

DARK CLOUDS ROLLED in the sky as Breeze headed back to the apothecary. The wind bringing the storm pulled at Breeze's skirts and flung her hair in her face. A bright flash lit the sky as Mother Nature cracked her whip. At obedience to her signal, cold, fat raindrops flung themselves down. Breeze began searching for a way to escape the sudden downpour. The town's little church, nestled between two larger buildings on the other side of the street, called out to her. She dashed across the street, almost losing her footing on the slick cobblestones, and slipped through the doorway into the safety of the church.

Once inside, Breeze immediately relaxed and took a deep breath. She loved this little old church. She loved the familiar scent of wooden benches and candles. She loved the simple wooden statues of the saints snuggled in their alcoves and the plain wooden cross hanging in the center flanked by carved angles with outstretched arms. Most of all she loved Father Paul. His sermons had always been delivered quietly. One might even say they were a touch dry, but Breeze found that if you made the effort to really listen you would hear the wisdom in his words. More often than not, she came away from meetings with a greater sense of peace than when she came into them.

Father Paul came shuffling up the center aisle to greet her, his threadbare purple shawl draped across his bony, drooping shoulders. He was so old she was afraid he would die before he reached the last pew. She moved forward to meet him. She wasn't sure how he was still living, but she was so grateful he was. If Drake's Uncle, Lord Hadrian, was the head of the town, Father Paul was its heart. He had been at the center of their lives, their births, marriages, deaths and all the little moments in between for so long it seemed that all their lives would stop when his did.

"Breeze, my dear girl, what a blessing. Storm drive you in, eh?" He held both his hands out to her and she took them, rubbing the paper-thin skin stretched over his swollen knuckles.

"No, of course not. I came here just to see you."

His laugh was so soft it was barely audible, but a sweet smile spread across his wrinkly face.

"Well, someone has already beat you to it," he informed her.

Breeze looked up and saw Boulder standing in front of the crackling fire, a stick of wood in his right hand and his left hand resting on the stone mantle. In his old age, Father Paul had gone the way of the reptile and could no longer hold his own body heat, so the townsfolk took turns keeping his fire going in all except the hottest months.

Breeze was glad for the opportunity to make amends for this morning and find out what Boulder had come into the shop for. Taking Breeze by the arm, Father Paul began the slow trek back down the short aisle. Boulder still hadn't noticed Breeze. He was staring intently at the simple wooden carving of the crucifixion above the fireplace. His brows were drawn together, and he seemed lost in thought.

"Boulder, my dear boy," Father Paul began, breaking Boulder's reverie. "The storm drove Breeze into the church. Isn't that a lovely coincidence? Now, I need to sit down again and study the good book, so I'm going to leave you two good, good friends alone."

With that he shuffled his way to his cozy sitting room at the back of the church.

"You seem deep in thought," Breeze commented.

Boulder's gaze was friendly but distracted.

"I was thinking about love," he explained.

Searching Boulder's face, she found no awkwardness there. She decided he must not be talking about the kind of love between gallant knights and beautiful ladies.

"We are asked to pray for those that hurt us and bless those that revile us but…do you think you could be happy loving like that?"

Even though she and Boulder had been born just a few weeks apart, Breeze felt suddenly childish.

"I-I don't really know," she stammered, "I have never really thought that much about it." She decided to change the subject.

"Will you and your father bring your tent to the tournament tomorrow?"

"We will. You and your father will be there as well as I presume?"

"We will."

"Ironic, isn't it? My craft makes your craft harder."

"How so?"

"It's the weapons I create which makes the wounds you heal." Boulder's brown eyes twinkled down at her.

"Well it's the knights themselves and all their fighting that will help put food on both our tables tomorrow," Breeze responded and they both smiled.

"I never found out why you came into the shop this morning. I'm sorry I was in such a hurry to leave."

Boulder gave her a half smile which she knew so well. "I forgive you." The words were effortlessly given but Breeze knew they came from a place of sincerity. For a moment the two friends stood staring at each other. An expression that Breeze couldn't read passed almost imperceptibly across Boulder's face. She opened her mouth to ask him about it, but he spoke first.

"Come," he said, taking Breeze's hand and putting it on the inside of his arm. "The rain stopped. I will walk you home."

"Thank you. We can get whatever it is that you were looking for."

"It's that nasty garlic drink. My dad is sick and he wants some. I think I would rather be sick than drink that stuff."

"It's not so bad when you put a little honey in it," Breeze suggested, laughing.

"There is not enough honey in this entire town to make garlic taste like something I would want to drink."

Chapter Five

BREEZE LEANED AGAINST the wooden post of their small tent, watching the sun descend in a blaze of orange and pink. She knew the mess she would find scattered across the table inside the tent and she didn't want to look. It made her tired just thinking about it. All tournaments were barely contained chaos at the apothecary's tent but this one had been particularly long. Some of the problems the knights came to her father with during these tournaments made her think they expected him to be a god instead of just an apothecary.

Looking down the aisle of tents she saw sparks fly in the descending darkness and heard Boulder's hammer ring out as he fixed yet another horseshoe for an anxiously pacing knight. She saw Drake and Aldwin passing Boulder's tent and her heart skipped a beat. She tucked loose hair behind her ears and attempted to smooth her tired looking apron. Drake leaned over and said something to Aldwin, who changed directions and disappeared down another line of tents.

As Drake drew nearer she asked, "What brings you over here?"

Drake held out his left hand to show a rapidly swelling knuckle.

"I'm sorry, my father is away from the tent attending to someone else. You will need to wait till he gets back."

Lifting one corner of his mouth in a slight smile Drake responded, "It's not your father I want to see."

"Well, uh," she stammered, thrilling at his attention, "Come inside and I will see what I can do for you."

The inside of the tent had barely enough room for the center table where she and her father worked on the knights and the smaller table against the tent wall which held all their supplies.

"I thought you weren't allowed to compete in the tournaments until after you are knighted," Breeze asked, surreptitiously trying to straighten up the work table.

"This didn't happen in a tournament," Drake replied nonchalantly, hopping up to sit on the other table. "Another squire and I had a disagreement that needed to be settled with our fists."

"That sounds like an intelligent solution," Breeze quipped.

He laughed again. Oh, that laugh. It was deep, vibrant, and unmistakable. Breeze wanted to do something more so she could hear it over and over again.

"Never fear, my lady, my uncle will be knighting me next week," he informed her, giving a low bow from the waist.

"Congratulations, Drake! That's wonderful news," Breeze responded, turning around and adopting her most officious tone. "Does this mean you are ready to live by the knight's code of chivalry? Are you ready to avoid all deceit, be loyal to God and country, and act gallantly toward women?"

"Oh, I don't bother with all that," he responded, waving a hand in the air. "No one ever won a tournament abiding by the code of conduct. It's the fighting, and of course the winning, that matters. That is what will give me the money, and therefore the freedom, I need. However, to do that, I need to be whole. Can you fix me?"

"If only I could," she replied, "but some things are beyond repair."

That earned her another laugh and this time she responded with a smile of her own.

"Will you at least try?" Seated on the table as he was their heads were perfectly level with each other. A strong impulse to lean her head forward and press her lips to his washed over her. It felt as if his inviting gaze were pulling her forward, but she didn't dare. Who was she to think she could kiss Drake McArthur?

"What if I try and I fail?"

"Then it will be the most pleasant failure I have ever experienced."

Could she just stay here forever with this beautiful man saying such sweet things to her? Was there more in life to be desired than moments like this?

"Then I will give everything I have to the task," she responded.

Stepping away from Drake she grabbed a bottle of wine and began pouring it into a small bowl of dried plantain.

"Are we celebrating?" Drake asked playfully, seeing the wine.

Breeze raised one eyebrow. "Celebrate? And what would we celebrate? The impulsivity and reckless behavior that landed you here in the first place? No. We are not celebrating. When you have learned to solve your problems with your words and your wisdom, come back and tell me. We'll celebrate then."

"Why would I do that?" Drake asked. "My sins seem to have led me to a happy ending so far."

His gaze upon her was so intense, she prayed silently her hands would be steady for the work. Breeze grabbed Drake's left hand and began gingerly straightening his fingers to check for breaks.

Drake winced and muttered something under his breath.

"Are you complaining?" Breeze asked with mock surprise.

"Are you touching me?" Drake responded, trying not to show his pain.

"Uh…yes."

"Then I'm not complaining."

Breeze cleared her throat and tried to get her heart rhythm to return to some semblance of normal as she began covering the swollen knuckle with the poultice. Grabbing a clean roll of linen from her apron she began expertly wrapping the poultice. She tucked the end of the linen neatly away and moved to release Drake's hand but he snatched up her hand with his good one.

As he pulled her forward he said, "I think I need you to bandage it a little more."

"That really isn't necessary," she responded weakly.

"Isn't it?"

His breath mingled with her own as she succumbed to the gravity that was pulling her forward.

"Another patient I see."

Her father's weary voice shattered the moment as well as her nerves. Whatever magnet had been pulling them forward instantly reversed itself at her father's appearance. Drake jumped off the table and Breeze spun around, instantly dedicating herself to studying the fascinating patterns of wood grain on the supply table.

She could just picture her father turning his head to one side trying to figure out why he could hear his daughter's beating heart or why her face was several shades off normal. But her father only tugged wearily at his wild hair.

"Sit, Drake," he commanded in a tired voice. "For tournaments that are supposed to be for fun and practice you knights certainly keep an old apothecary moving."

"I actually think it's all healed," Drake declared, holding up his bandaged hand. With a curt nod in Breeze's direction, he muttered a polite thank you and cleared the tent door in less than two strides. Galen looked back and forth from his daughter to the empty doorway as if trying to diagnose the situation and prescribe the cure.

Finally, he shrugged his shoulders. "Under normal circumstances I would wonder why he is acting so odd, but right now, I am too tired to care. Let's go home."

Chapter Six

Early summer was pouring its warm goodwill on the people of Northwell. Breeze stood in the doorway of the shop watching people pass by. Friends stood longer than usual talking in the street and children danced about with arms outstretched and faces upturned, unabashedly receiving the gift of summer sunshine.

"Breeze, will you join me in the back for a moment," Galen asked.

Breeze reluctantly agreed. She knew what this conversation was going to be about and she did not want to have it. Ever since the tournament, Drake had been finding reasons to visit the shop and each time he would leave her a letter. He would tell her all about his life at the castle and his dreams of becoming a knight. She would find a way to send one back, usually through Aldwin. Since she and Caroline had not spoken since the day at the bakery, Breeze was able to occasionally lie and tell her parents she was going for a walk with Caroline, and then sneak out for a walk with Drake. She hated lying to her parents, especially her dad, but she couldn't see any other options. She wasn't sure why Drake was being so secretive about their growing friendship but she didn't dare question him and risk ruining their relationship.

Considering his behavior at the tournament, Breeze felt confused by how platonic their relationship had become. His conversations were always engaged and lively but he rarely touched her in any way except for a goodnight hug at the end of their walks. Even though she yearned for more, she was grateful that she had his attention at all. Each letter they wrote and each walk they took was a thread weaving her life-long dream into a reality.

A variety of herbs were piled high on the table in the center of the room and she knew her father had been harvesting in the garden. She picked up a few sprigs of mint and inhaled deeply, savoring the scent, and then began searching for a ball of twine on the cluttered counter against the wall.

"Dad, how do you find anything in here?" Breeze asked, exasperated.

Galen picked up the ball of twine which had been right next to him on the bench and raised an eyebrow at Breeze. Without saying anything Breeze sat on the bench beside her father and took the ball of twine. For a while they both worked in silence, losing themselves in the scent and feel of freshly cut herbs. Then Galen broke the silence.

"Drake seems to be coming around more often."

Breeze just nodded her head, unwilling to give an audible answer.

"He is definitely very handsome," her father tried again.

Breeze shifted uncomfortably and didn't respond at all this time since it wasn't actually a question.

"There is some gossip coming through the shop about Drake, and not all of it is favorable."

"Father, haven't you been telling me since I was a little girl to be cautious about believing the things I hear in the shop," Breeze responded, standing up with a bundle of mint.

Galen decided to change tactics. "Boulder's father and I had always hoped that maybe you and Boulder would make a good match."

With intentional silence, Breeze turned her back on her father as she climbed on a stool to hang the mint leaves from a ceiling beam.

Undeterred, Galen tried again. "I may be an old man, Breeze, but it seems to me that when Boulder passes through he causes quite the stir among the young ladies in the town."

That brought Breeze's head around. With a sigh she succumbed to the conversation since she could tell she wasn't getting out of here without talking about what her father wanted to talk about. She climbed down from the stool and began arranging another handful of herbs into a bundle.

"Boulder is nice to look at, no doubt about that, and his body is—" Breeze glanced over and saw her father's eyes widen and color flush his cheeks. "Well, it's sufficient to get a day's work done," she finished lamely. "But Boulder is like…earth. He is something solid to stand on. Drake on the other hand, he is like *fire*." She breathed the last word out in an excited whisper. "When I am around him I can feel all my senses are awake, eagerly waiting for the next moment to occur."

"Fire, huh?" Her dad's head was down, his brows drawn together and his mouth pulled down in the corners in a thoughtful frown. His hands moved methodically, wrapping twine around the stems of a bundle of lavender. Looking up his eyes rested on the fire at the far end of the workroom. For a moment he was frozen in thoughtful silence. Breeze wasn't sure she wanted to know what her father was thinking. The wood crackled in the fireplace, doing a much better job than Breeze of upholding its end of the conversation.

"Fire in its place, contained by stones or walls, is a marvelous thing. Fire gives light, life, and warmth to those who use it. Life without fire would be hard indeed." At this he moved his gaze to the hills, which in just a few short months would brown under the late summer sun, "But a fire without limits, a fire that is allowed to burn free without restraint upon fuel that is ready to burn, that helps no one, and destroys all who get in its way."

She looked up at him now and he pulled his gaze back to stare directly into her eyes. "Be careful with fire, Breeze. It can give you warmth and light, or it can consume you."

Galen let the silence hang in the air for a time while Breeze chewed over that thought in her mind.

"Seems to me," Galen continued, "of what I have heard of Drake he is more the later kind of fire than the former."

Anger flared within Breeze.

"You don't know him, Dad," she snapped.

Galen didn't rise to the bait, but stayed calm.

"Neither do you, Breeze. Neither do you."

Chapter Seven

BREEZE SHIVERED AND clutched the shawl more tightly around herself as she hurried toward the church with the wood for Father Paul's fire. It was an unusually chilly midsummer night and she berated herself for waiting so late in the day to bring Father Paul his wood. The press of duties at the apothecary distracted her until she felt the chill of the night air creeping in. Her heart had dropped like a stone when she remembered that it was her family's turn to tend to the fire at the church.

Stepping into the church, she was momentarily blinded by the darkness. She was even more angry with herself when she saw the dying coals in the fireplace where a burning fire should have been. Racing up the aisle toward the fireplace she screamed when she felt a hand grab her skirt. The wood fell to the floor with a deafening clatter. And then she heard the laughter. She knew that sound.

"Drake! What are you doing here?" Breeze was gasping for breath with her hand pressed hard against her racing heart.

"You're going to wake Father Paul with all that racket," he responded calmly as if nothing out of the ordinary had happened. "Besides, I am supposed to be here…all night as a matter of fact." Breeze noticed a touch of resentment in the last words he spoke. "What are you doing here?"

"I'm here to bring the wood for Father Paul's fire."

"You mean for his coals?" he teased, and then he laughed again.

The comment stoked Breeze's guilt as well as her temper.

"A church isn't normally the kind of place I would expect to see you spending voluntary time," she retorted, "so tell me again why you are here?"

"It's not voluntary. I am being knighted tomorrow so, as is the custom, I must spend the night in prayer and meditation. Then in the morning I will bathe and prepare myself to be presented before my uncle."

"I knew you were being knighted tomorrow but you never said anything about needing to spend the night in the church."

Drake stood and stepped out of the pew. "Well, it's a dumb custom. It hardly seemed worth mentioning."

He lowered his voice and pulled Breeze's body closer to his. "I'll be thinking of you tonight."

Breeze became keenly aware that except for a nearly deaf and nearly dead priest in the next room they were completely alone in the darkness.

"I thought you just said you were supposed to be thinking about God?" she whispered back, her heart racing for an entirely new reason.

"Perhaps, but the night will pass so much more pleasantly if I am thinking of you." He leaned down and softly rubbed the end of his nose against hers.

"How about I do the praying for you then," she suggested, trying desperately to dispel the flood of passion she felt rising within her. Oh, how she had wanted this kind of attention from him! But not here! Not in her beloved church.

"God will surely be more willing to listen to an angel such as yourself than a devil like me," he responded, lightly placing his fingertips on her temple. Slowly, he slid his fingers around the curve of her face. When his fingers reached her chin he pushed up slightly, lifting her lips to his. The kiss was soft but not weak, firm but not hard. It pulled her in and she surrendered. She felt a great cosmic click as if the universe itself aligned to show her that she was exactly where she belonged. Never before had she had such an overwhelming feeling that something was right. But she also knew that this was not the time or place to get swept away in a torrent of passion.

"Well," she uttered, after breaking the kiss. She could feel her heart, which had completely lost its rhythm, beating erratically. Her breath caught slightly in her throat on each inhale. The whirlwind inside her mind was threatening to blow away her last rational thought.

"Well," she tried again, a little stronger this time," if you won't be praying tonight, I had best get started."

With more internal strength than she knew she possessed she broke his embrace and hurriedly raced out of the church. Drake stood silent and still as he watched her go, the scattered firewood at his feet and behind him, the dying embers of the fire.

Chapter Eight

SUMMER WAS DRAWING to a close, but not with a gentle good-bye. It was racing towards the end by pushing all its energy into this single, sweltering day. Sweat trickled down Breeze's back as she sat in the hard pew of Father Paul's church. Being sandwiched between her father on one side and Boulder on the other wasn't helping the situation. But their families had sat in the same pew for as long as she could remember, and a hot day wouldn't change that. Father Paul was delivering what Breeze was sure was a lovely sermon but all she could think about was Drake. Breeze had heard from the nobles and wealthy merchants that came through the shop about Drake receiving his knighthood. Shortly after the ceremony, he had taken off with Balius and Aldwin, his newly appointed squire, to compete in as many tournaments as he possibly could. If rumor could be believed, he was winning far more than he was losing.

When Breeze was being honest with herself his silence toward her hurt. She was embarrassed to admit how distracted she had been since their kiss, how much time she spent daydreaming about him.

And now he was here and she hated it. Normally she loved coming to church. It was a time when the townsfolk laid aside their work and gathered together. There was much visiting and laughter outside the church's wooden doors as friends greeted one another. Breeze also enjoyed

Father Paul's sermons. She found that life seemed to go a little better when she made an effort to do the things he taught.

But today she wanted to run. From her view in the middle of the church where all the tradesman sat she could see Lord Hadrian and the nobility. To Lord Hadrian's left sat Drake, and to Drake's left sat Elaine. Drake's broad shoulders were framed perfectly by his velvet green coat. Elaine's glossy black hair coiled in braids above her graceful white neck which was encircled by the lacey white collar of her blue silk dress. There were mere inches separating their shoulders. Breeze felt nauseous with jealousy. As she sat trying to calm her pounding heart, Father Paul shuffled to the front of the church and up to the podium. Normally he carried a parchment or a scroll with his sermon carefully scratched out with quill and ink. Today, however, he placed his hands on either side of the podium, looked out upon the congregation, and started speaking.

"God has asked us to put him in the center of our lives," he intoned.

Breeze could barely hear Father Paul's words. The questions flooding her mind crowded out any other thought.

How long has he been in town? Did he go to see her first? Why didn't he come to see me?

"...to treasure Him and to love Him above all else."

Everyone was shifting uncomfortably in their seats, trying to dissipate some of the heat.

"...but why has He asked this of us? Because He is selfish?"

Breeze noticed that Drake kept lifting his hand to his back and scratching it in a weird way. *Why was he doing that?*

"No. Because he wants us to be happy."

With a start Breeze noticed that Drake was actually spelling letters on his back. She saw him look up and to the side as if contemplating the small wooden carvings of the saints but she knew he was looking to see if she understood. She cleared her throat ever so slightly to show him that she did.

"God knows he is the only one who can love us perfectly…"

Drake began again to spell the letters on his back.

I…a…m

Breeze put the letters together.

I am

"and so our whole hearts can only be safe in his hands."

T…h…i…n

I am thin? What? Was he serious?

"When we put others in the center of our lives then like the spokes of a wheel they can tell us how to act, what to believe, and how to feel, especially how to feel about ourselves."

K…i…n…g

I am thin king? This doesn't make any sense at all. He is just teasing me… Oh! I am thinking!

"Consider the glorious image of the Savior on the cross. He loved others perfectly but because His Father was always in His center, He did not allow others' treatment of Him to affect his worth."

What? What are you thinking of?

"He always remembered who He was and how His Father felt about Him."

Ugh! Father Paul will you please just stop talking! I can't concentrate!

o…f…

Breeze's heart was racing in anticipation.

y…o…u

Of you. Of me.

Her racing heart dropped to the floor with contentment. Father Paul's words floated harmlessly by without disturbing the peaceful feeling she now held in her heart.

"May we always have the courage to keep God in the center of our lives is my humble prayer."

R…

Wait! He was still writing…your…

L…i…p…s

Your lips.

For reasons Breeze couldn't explain her heart ached a little. She wished he had stopped at "you". It felt sweeter to her that way.

"In the name of the Father, of the Son, and of the Holy Ghost. Amen."

All the townsfolk were eager to escape the sweltering church but remained seated so Lord Hadrian and his party could leave first. As Breeze waited, she puzzled over how she felt. After all, she had really enjoyed the kiss, too. She was still staring at Drake's back when she saw Elaine turn and whisper something in Drake's ear. Whatever she said made Drake laugh and she laid her head briefly against his shoulder. When Drake stood to follow his uncle, he reached out his hand for Elaine and helped her to her feet. When she stood, Drake leaned down and whispered something in her ear in return. They both laughed as he lifted her hand to his mouth, kissed her fingers and then placed her hand on his arm to escort her out of the church.

Breeze felt cold as she watched their retreating backs.

"That was a really good sermon, don't you think?" Boulder asked. "It answered some of my questions about love."

"If you know so much about love," Breeze retorted, "tell me why I've spent my whole life loving someone I can't have."

Boulder laid a comforting arm around Breeze's shoulders. "I'm sorry," he said, "It must be hard to watch the two of them together. Would you like me to walk you home?"

"No, thank you. I just want to be alone."

Chapter Nine

BREEZE LAY AWAKE in her bed, unable to sleep. Scenes from the day replayed over and over in her mind and her heart soared and dropped, soared and dropped, again and again just as it had at the church. She sat propped up in bed staring at the wooden floorboards where the full moon shone in through her open window. With each passing minute that the day's events chased sleep from her eyes she became angrier and angrier at Drake.

The clopping of hooves sounded outside her bedroom window. Then Drake's voice called out in a whisper, "Breeze!...Breeze!"

What in name of all that was good and holy was Drake doing outside her window? Breeze crossed her arms and pressed herself further into her bed. It didn't matter what he was doing, she wasn't going to answer.

"Breeze...!" then louder, "Breeze!"

Breeze raced to the window.

"Drake MacArthur, be quiet! You are going to wake up my parents and everyone else on this street."

Drake just smiled his perfect smile up at her, his long, wavy black hair falling down his shoulders and his emerald green eyes reflecting the light of the moon. Beneath him, Balius shifted lazily from one hoof to the other.

"You look lovely in the moonlight."

Breeze could feel the grip on her righteous anger slipping. How could you stay angry at someone who was looking at you like that? Then she remembered Elaine and her anger flared again.

Breeze adopted her sweetest voice, "Mighty champion, you seem to be lost. Elaine's home is that way." She gestured towards Elaine's manor with a toss of her head, stormed back into her room, and flung herself onto her bed.

To her surprise and extreme agitation, she heard him laugh.

"Breeze!" he called again with no hint of a whisper.

She raced back to the window.

"Go away!" she hissed.

"Gladly, my heart, as long as you come with me."

"Why would I go anywhere with you?"

He grew quiet and sincere. "I would love to tell you that if you will give me a chance. Come, go for a ride with me."

"In the middle of the night?" Breeze felt torn. Part of her wanted to leap out the window and ride off into the cool night air with Drake but another part of her felt foolish for so quickly abandoning her anger.

"The moon is so bright you can't look at it straight on. We will easily see where we are going."

She hesitated only a moment longer. Her curiosity about what Drake would say combined with her love of the peacefulness of night eroded the last of her anger.

After grabbing her cloak and hood, Breeze swung her leg over the window and lowered herself into Drake's waiting arms. She deliberately turned her face forward and said, "I'm only doing this because I want to see the stars." Drake didn't bother mentioning that the brightness of the moon made this a poor night to see stars. He just chuckled deeply, which Breeze felt through her back, and clicked softly to Balius to walk on.

"Where are we going?" Breeze asked. The gentle sway of Balius' slow walk and the warmth of Drake's chest had the effect of causing her to relax despite her determination to hold onto her indignation.

"The overlook by Cob's Hill. I thought this would be a nice night to see our little valley bathed in moonlight."

They rode on in silence, savoring the soft night breeze, the friendly chirping of crickets, the croaking of frogs, and most of all the warm comforting presence of each other. When they reached the overlook, they dismounted and moved to a large stone—the perfect place to rest and look down on their small, sleeping town. Drake sat next to Breeze, repeatedly lifting strands of hair from the back of her head and running his fingers all the way to the bottom. The effect on Breeze was like a magical potion. She could feel her whole body falling into a trance-like state.

"Are you going to tell me why you were so angry with me after I came out in the middle of the night because I so desperately wanted to see you?"

Breeze really didn't want to remember why she was so angry, much less talk about it. She wanted to stay nestled under the cover of night with Drake's strong, warm body by her side.

She simply shrugged. "I don't know."

"You said something about Elaine?" Drake prodded and Breeze could hear the smile in his voice, almost like he was teasing her.

She decided to just be honest. "After our…" she found that she was too embarrassed to say the word kiss, "our night at the church, I felt jealous when I saw you courting Elaine today in church."

Drake's laughter, normally such a magical sound for her, stung.

He moved around so he was kneeling in front of her on the rock. He took her face in both of his hands and looked intently into her eyes.

"I was not courting Elaine today."

"I know what I saw, Drake."

He paused before answering, caressing her eyebrows with his thumbs and leaning in to kiss her forehead. Drawing back, he looked directly in her eyes.

"Whatever you think you may have seen, I was not courting Elaine today."

"You smiled at her, whispered in her ear and kissed her hand. If a man treated me that way I would call it courting."

"What would you have me do? Never speak to Elaine again?"

"No, of course not." It was almost a whisper. In truth she would have loved that and it made her feel mean and small to admit it. She wished she had never said anything about it.

Drake moved his hands down to rest lightly on her neck and began stroking her jawline with his thumb as he spoke.

"I wanted to talk to you about something. Maybe you know that I have been winning a lot of tournaments lately."

Breeze wasn't sure where Drake was going with this.

"Yes, I have heard."

Drake seemed nervous and it surprised Breeze.

"If I keep winning like I am now, I will be able to become independent from my uncle."

Breeze remembered a conversation from a few months back and with it a thought began to form and a hope tried to attach itself to that thought, but Breeze shook them both off.

Drake took both her hands in his.

"Breeze, will you marry me?"

Annoyed, Breeze let go of his hands.

"Don't tease me, Drake. It isn't kind. My heart isn't a toy for you to play with."

The semi-dark of the night made it difficult to fully read Drake's expression.

"Why do you think I am teasing you?" His voice was even, betraying nothing.

"You are intended for Elaine. Beautiful. Perfect. Elaine."

"Do you not think you are beautiful?"

"I think it's irrelevant. Beauty doesn't heal wounds and cure fevers."

"Exactly. That's one of the things I love about you."

All Breeze's senses became sharply alert. *Did he just say that he loved me?*

"You're useful. You have skills and you help people. Yes, Elaine is beautiful but that's all she is. I want to come home to more than just talk of jewels and dresses each day. Besides," he smiled at her, "what could be a more perfect fit than a wound prone knight and a skilled apothecary?"

"But what about Elaine? I saw the way she looked at you today. She adores you."

"Elaine wants nothing more than to hang me on her wall as a trophy to show off to all her friends. I need more than that for my life. I want to live a life of purpose and meaning. A life that I choose, not one that is chosen for me. And I choose you, Breeze. I...I felt something the day I kissed you in the church. Did you not feel it?"

Breeze looked at Drake in surprise. She had never talked to Drake about their kiss so she didn't know that he had felt the same thing.

"Yes," she whispered, as if speaking any louder would shatter the reality of this moment.

"What more do you need?" he asked, leaning forward and nuzzling her ear with his nose. "Marry me."

She turned towards him and their lips met. She felt a wave of desire and there it was again. A feeling that felt like home in a different way than she had ever experienced it and she knew, with every part of her she knew, she wanted this. She wanted to be right here, next to Drake McArthur, for the rest of her life.

"Yes," she breathed, their lips still lightly touching.

He immediately pulled her to her feet and wrapped her in his arms.

"I have a place we can go tonight to consummate the marriage. Breeze, you have made me the happiest of men! After my mom died I never thought I would experience this kind of happiness again. Come, I can't wait." Drake reached for Breeze's wrist and began leading her toward the horse.

"Wait! Wait! You meant tonight?"

Drake looked genuinely surprised by her reluctance. "You know the law as well as I. Two people only need agree with each other and then…well, then seal the marriage with their bodies for the marriage to be binding."

"I do know the law but," Breeze paused, feeling timid. "I was hoping to have Father Paul perform the marriage and, of course, I would want my parents there."

"Do you think that's wise to tell your parents before it happens? Seems to me that telling your parents would guarantee the marriage wouldn't happen."

Breeze couldn't deny the truth of that.

Drake leaned in and kissed her again more deeply this time, pouring all the passion he felt into that single kiss.

"Breeze, my beautiful girl, now that I know you will have me, I couldn't bear it if it didn't happen."

Breeze felt that same torrent of passion she felt in the church, demanding that she succumb, but there was another part of her, small but tenacious, that knew she wanted at least one witness at her wedding.

"Drake, I will marry you, I promise. There is nothing I want more. And I won't tell my parents. But, I do want Father Paul to perform a ceremony. I know the law doesn't require it, but I wish it."

"If you wish it, then I can grant it. I will arrange things with Father Paul tomorrow and then send word for you to come meet me at the church."

Chapter Ten

BREEZE WOKE BEFORE dawn, her heart racing the moment she opened her eyes. Sitting up, she quickly donned her dress and then sat back down and began carefully pulling her wooden comb through her long, silky hair. Each time she pulled the comb through her hair she dipped it in a bowl of rose water sitting next to her bed until her hair fell shining and rose-scented down her back. Shivers went through her body as she thought that before the sun set again this day Drake would be running his hands through her hair.

She tied it with a simple ribbon at the nape of her neck. She knew her parents would suspect something if she wore it down to work in the shop but she also knew she wanted to be able to let it down for the ceremony as the symbol of her purity.

The morning sun crept through her window and laid itself across her floor. She knew it was safe to go downstairs without questions about why she was up so early.

The day began its painfully slow journey. Every moment felt like an hour. Every customer that walked into the shop set her nerves on fire with anticipation. The sun climbed all the way up to its peak and was almost done with its slow descent back toward the earth. There still had been no word from Drake.

Breeze was in the back room asking her dad for some fennel tea to calm her stomach, which had had enough of the day's turbulence, when she heard footsteps in the front room. As it had been doing all day, her heart leapt into her throat and started pounding away as she walked into the shop.

She was immediately disappointed. Of all the people she knew Drake would not send word by, Caroline was definitely one of them.

"Hi, Caroline." The disappointment in her voice was obvious but Breeze was too consumed with worry to see her friend's hurt expression.

"My little sister has an ear infection."

"Let me get the mullein oil," Breeze said flatly and turned to grab the bottle from its usual place on the shelf. It wasn't there. Amber glass bottles were scattered haphazardly across the shelves."

"It isn't here," Breeze said, flustered. "I will just make some but you will need to wait a few hours to put it in her ear so it has time steep. It should be ready by bedtime," she instructed, opening a drawer beneath the counter labeled "mullein" in neatly penned letters. She expected to see dried mullein flowers, but it was also empty. Why was it empty?

"Just a moment, Caroline, let me ask my dad what to do."

As Breeze walked into the backroom her mind turned back to Drake. *What if he is just playing with me? What if he changed his mind? What if he realized how foolish it would be to marry me, Breeze, the simple apothecary's daughter, when he could have wealthy, beautiful Elaine?*

"Dad, we are out of mullein oil and flowers but Caroline's sister has an ear infection. What should I do?"

Galen drew his brows together over his haggard eyes and responded in a tired voice, "You know as well as I that garlic oil also works."

Breeze stared at her father, slightly confused. She did know that. Why had she come back here to ask him when she already knew the answer? Shaking her head, she went through the door back into the shop.

"Caroline, how is your family doing?" Breeze asked politely. In truth, she really didn't care at this moment but it would buy her time to search desperately for the garlic oil.

"We are fine, thank you," was Caroline's curt reply.

"That's lovely," was Breeze's distracted answer as she rummaged through bottles, bowls, and drawers. Success! She snatched the garlic oil from the corner it was hiding in and handed it to Caroline, who began opening her purse.

"No," Breeze said, truly looking at her friend now. "Please, from our family to yours. I hope your sister feels better."

Caroline looked pointedly at Breeze as she finished drawing the copper coin from her pouch and laid it on the counter.

"Thank you for the oil," she replied as she picked up the bottle and left the shop.

Just as the sun disappeared behind the row of houses across the street, Aldwin appeared in the shop. The sun seemed to have set on Aldwin's face as well. Breeze had never seen him looking so grave. The tension etched into every line of his face did nothing to soothe Breeze's frazzled nerves. He held out an envelope and then retreated without a word.

Breeze quickly left the shop, racing up the stairs to the safety of her room. The envelope trembled in her hands and she feared to open it, but she couldn't just stand there wondering. She opened it.

My Dearest Breeze,

I am waiting for you. Come now.

Her heart soared. She wanted to scream for joy but knew she couldn't. But how to get there? She looked around. She couldn't go out the front door. She felt another stab of shame about deceiving her parents but she knew Drake was right. They were meant to be together and telling her parents could jeopardize that. She would tell them as soon as it was over and she and Drake were irrefutably husband and wife. Her heart rejoiced at the thought. She had to find a way down! The window on the street side was too high without Balius and Drake there to catch her. The window overlooking the garden had a low thatched roof beneath it that she could easily walk down and then drop into the garden.

In a moment, she was racing down the street toward the church. She knew that running would draw attention she probably didn't want at this moment but she couldn't help it. A dream she had longed for since childhood was about to come true and she needed to get there as fast as she could.

She burst through the door of the church and immediately heard his laughter, a joyous, wonderful sound. A sound she was going to get to hear, God willing, for the rest of her life. He caught her up in his arms, spun her around, and then kissed her passionately before setting her down. The moment her feet touched the floor she noticed Father Paul and blushed deeply that he had been a witness to their unrestrained display.

She walked up to the beloved old man and took his wrinkled, bony hands in hers. "Father Paul, thank you so much for being willing to do a small ceremony for us. It means so much to me."

"Did you not want your parents to be here?" he asked, a look of concern on his face.

The question stung and she felt a small flash of anger at Father Paul for asking it. Did no one understand their joy?

"They don't understand what I want," she replied with her chin up and her shoulders back.

"Do you know that this is what you want?" He asked so harmlessly that Breeze couldn't be angry at him anymore. She knew how much he loved her.

"Yes. I know this is what I want more than I have ever known anything."

"Well, then, let's get started."

Drake, who had been watching the whole conversation from a few feet away came and stood beside Breeze.

Father Paul began, "Marriage is the most important decision you will ever make."

Breeze was surprised to hear Drake chuckling quietly. She elbowed him playfully in the ribs. Father Paul paused and looked back and forth from bride to groom, concern clearly written on his face.

"Drake, will you take Breeze to be thy wedded wife, to live together in the holy order of matrimony? Will you love her, comfort her, honor, and keep her, in sickness and in health; and forsaking all others, keeping her only unto you, so long as you both shall live?"

"I will."

Breeze knew she would never be able to describe the way she felt when he said those two simple words. She felt the promise of them in his gaze and heard the truth of them in his voice. For the first time all day, her heart was at peace.

"Breeze, will you take Drake to be your wedded husband, to live together in the holy order of Matrimony? Will you love him, comfort him, honor him, and keep him, in sickness and in heath, forsaking all others, keeping him only to you, so long as you both shall live."

"I will." And she knew that she would. She knew that, no matter what, she would never walk away from this man.

"Then I pronounce you husband and wife. You may kiss the bride, but Drake, keep it chaste. This is a church."

Breeze and Drake obediently kissed each other with a brief touch of the lips. "Now, if you two lovebirds want to wait a moment I can give you an official certificate with my seal on it." Breeze looked up at Drake and saw the hunger in his eyes and it thrilled her.

"No, thank you, Father Paul. It's getting late and we had best set out." She gave him a quick hug. "But thank you, so much."

Holding hands, Breeze and Drake stepped out of the church into the darkness of the night, eager to seal the marriage and become one.

Chapter Eleven

J UST LIKE THE morning before, Breeze sat on the side of the bed, but everything else was different. She was no longer simply Breeze, the apothecary's daughter. Now she was Breeze, the wife of Sir Drake McArthur. Her heart swelled with pride at the thought as her fingers worked to pull the tangles out of her hair. What would Caroline say? She couldn't wait to tell her.

She looked around at the place they had used to finish the wedding ceremony, an old, abandoned shed in the woods just outside the castle grounds. Drake had spent the entire day cleaning it out and preparing it for Breeze; fixing boards, thatching the roof, sweeping the floor, and making a bed of hay and furs taken from the castle. A stone fireplace stood in center of the room with a freshly chopped supply of firewood piled in the corner.

Breeze didn't see much of the shed last night because it was so dark but she saw it now and it made her grateful all over again for the decision she had made. She was eager to go tell her parents as soon as she got the unruly mess on her head under control. She knew when they saw her joy they would understand.

She heard Drake shift in the bed behind her and she turned to look. His deep green eyes were open and resting on her face. She felt a flood of happiness as she remembered the moments they shared after their simple ceremony. He reached up and began lifting strands of her hair and running his fingers down them.

"Good morning, lovely."

"Good morning, my love." She leaned down and kissed him. These lips, this man, this was where she belonged now. She was going to be able to kiss this mouth over and over again as freely as she chose. The feeling this gave her was indescribable.

"I'm so excited to begin telling everyone, especially my parents. I hate that I left my dad yesterday without any explanation. I just have to get this tangled mess under control so I don't walk through town looking like I just had a hard night on the wine."

Drake pulled his brows together and Breeze noticed the corners of his beautiful mouth pull down.

"What's wrong, my love?" She leaned in again and kissed him adding, "my husband" and then smiled because it sounded so good.

"I think we should wait to announce the marriage."

Instantly, Breeze sat up.

"You said I could tell my parents as soon as we were married."

"I actually never said anything about telling your parents. I just asked if you thought it was wise to tell them beforehand. You were the one who said you wouldn't tell them."

Breeze stared hard at a patch of dirt on the floor. Her stomach, still not recovered from yesterday, twisted in knots.

"How long do you want to wait before we announce it?"

"I just need to build up some more of my own money first. When my Uncle finds out he will completely disown me. I need to be able to afford my own horse, weapons, and armor. If the tournaments are big and I win the joust it shouldn't take more than two or three more tournaments."

Breeze felt foolish and anxious. Why hadn't she thought of that before the ceremony? Why had she been so hasty? If they had just waited a couple more months she wouldn't have to keep so profound a secret from her parents, from Caroline, from everyone. But then she thought of last night. Could she really regret that? Marrying Drake was her childhood dream, and yesterday it came true. What was a few months of secrecy? Certainly, being married to Drake would be worth the sacrifice of a little lie here and there to keep their marriage a secret and ensure Drake was able to build a successful career as a knight.

"You're right," she said. "I can wait a little longer." She dreaded going home now. It was going to be so much harder to explain her abrupt departure yesterday as well as why she stayed out all night. She hated lying. It made her feel so distant from her parents. But she would think of something, she would manage it, for Drake. "I need to get back to the shop. Dad will be needing me."

"Wait," he said and pulled her in for a kiss. "Meet me here again tonight?"

"How if I can't tell my parents? How will I manage to leave?"

Drake smiled at her and tucked her hair behind her ear. "You're brilliant. I know you'll think of something." He kissed her again, longer this time. "Meet me tonight?"

"Yes," she agreed breathlessly. "I'll be here." She didn't know how, but she knew she would make it happen.

Chapter Twelve

SUMMER FINISHED ITS race, flopping painfully and swelteringly across the finish line, and Fall stepped in with fresh legs and a welcome breeze to cool everyone off.

The night after the wedding, Breeze had managed to come up with a lie about being detained at the home of someone on the outskirts of town who had fallen rapidly ill. She wasn't sure if her parents believed her but they didn't ask any more questions. From then Breeze had fallen into a routine of sneaking out after her parents were asleep, racing to Drake through the rustling of fallen leaves, and hurrying home again in the crisp morning air, her breath turning into icy clouds as she ran. The nights were more wonderful than anything Breeze could ever have imagined but the days were pure misery. Exhausted and distracted, her mind was rarely on her work. One moment she was yearning to lie down and sleep right on the wooden floor of the shop and the next she was yearning for the cover of night to fall so she could escape to the comfort, connection, and passion she felt in Drake's arms.

Waiting for Drake to earn enough money so she could announce the marriage publicly was almost unendurable. Fortunately, there would be a tournament in just a few days in a large town with a large sum for a prize. Breeze spent countless hours obsessing over how much armor, horses, and weapons cost, subjects she had never given a moment's notice to before. She had tried gleaning as much information from Aldwin as she could on the subject without raising too much suspicion by her interest. She spun her future with Drake in her mind a thousand different times in a thousand different ways. Maybe she could get work in another town as an apothecary and help support them. Maybe Drake could get hired by the Lord of a castle that would temporarily supply all his needs. Breeze knew that if she thought about it hard enough she could make all this tortuous waiting come to an end.

All of this obsessive thinking was not helping her work. After a bedraggled mother with a cranky newborn and an exuberant toddler had to repeat herself three times before Breeze could remember what she needed, she decided it was time to take a walk. "Dad, I'm leaving," she called to the back and without looking to see if her father heard her, she walked past the woman and out of the shop.

She immediately regretted leaving her cloak and began walking quickly without thought for her direction, just to dispel her pent-up energy and warm her shivering muscles. Within a few moments she noticed that her legs were taking her, out of habit she guessed, to the bakery. She slowed a little then, contemplating if she wouldn't rather be frozen by Mother Nature instead of Caroline. It was less personal when Mother Nature did it. After all, it wasn't as if she could say anything to Caroline. This thought made her feel so lonely. Before Drake she had always shared everything with her parents and with Caroline. She lived heart open to the world. But now that she had given her heart to Drake, she had to close it to everyone else. Her footsteps slowed as she wrapped her arms around herself. Maybe she didn't want to go see Caroline after all.

And then she heard his voice and her heart leapt up. It was coming from Caroline's shop! What a beautiful coincidence! Oh, how she needed him right now. Breeze was sure they could find just a few moments to slip away together, just so he could hold her in his arms and tell her how it was all going to be alright in the end. She honestly couldn't remember the last time she saw his face in the daylight.

Almost leaping the last few steps, Breeze flew around the corner of the shop and heard another woman's voice, too.

Elaine.

From the doorway Breeze could see her smiling up at Drake with her perfectly shaped mouth, her raven black hair falling down her back. Her dress of royal blue velvet perfectly reflected the pristine blue of her eyes, where Breeze saw that same mixture of adoration and ownership that had so sickened her at the church. Seeing the same look reflected in Drake's eyes was more than Breeze could handle. She felt a wave of fire and nausea. She heard Drake's voice as if from another room when he offered, "A sweet treat for a sweet lady," and then saw him hold up an apple tart for Elaine to try. Elaine lifted a hand and placed it under Drake's as he put the apple tart in her mouth. Their shared laughter was the most painful sound Breeze had ever heard.

It was then Caroline noticed Breeze. "Good day, Breeze. Can I get you something?"

Drake and Elaine turned their smiling faces on Breeze.

"Look, Elaine, it's Breeze," Drake said with perfect ease. "How are you today?"

Breeze didn't know what she expected but she knew that wasn't it. She stared hard at his face. There was not a single muscle out of place, no sign of tension or discomfort. An artist could have studied his face for hours and not found the slightest trace of evidence that Drake and Breeze were anything more than friendly acquaintances. His lack of discomfort was so complete that for a moment Breeze questioned whether she and Drake really were married and maybe she was dreaming it all up.

Elaine was looking at Breeze with a look of genuine concern which made Breeze hate her all the more.

Elaine asked, "Are you alright? You are not looking quite yourself."

Shame flooded Breeze as she became acutely aware of her appearance. Her hair and clothes were disheveled since she had little time to care for them in the morning as she raced home through the dark woods. Dark circles ringed her eyes from weeks of sleep deprivation. In contrast, Elaine's hair and dress were impeccable. Her flawless skin was the perfect backdrop for the slight blush of her cheeks, possibly brought on by the pleasure she felt at Drake's presence.

Breeze wanted to lash out at Drake but knew she couldn't without jeopardizing her own future.

"Elaine," she said sweetly, "are you sure you should be eating that apple tart? Isn't that a dark spot I see on your tooth?"

The hurt she saw in Elaine's eyes made Breeze hate herself, as well.

Turning to Drake, Elaine asked quietly, "Will you please escort me home?"

"With pleasure, my lady," Drake responded with all the gallant tenderness of a chivalrous knight. Drake took Elaine's right hand in his and put his left arm around her waist to lead her out of the shop. As he passed Breeze he glanced at her over Elaine's head with a look of pure rage.

Tears welled in her eyes as she stood frozen to the spot. When she finally looked up, she saw Caroline staring at her with confusion and concern.

"That was really mean," Caroline observed, "and not really like you. Will you tell me what's going on?"

Yes. Yes, a thousand times. She wanted to run into Caroline's arms and share everything with her and allow her friend to help carry her burden. But she couldn't. She had promised.

"No."

And then she turned and walked out of the shop.

Breeze didn't go to Drake that night, or the next, or the one after that and although she was getting more sleep, it didn't help her level of distraction in the shop. At one point her father became so frustrated at having to mitigate situations with angry customers, he sent her to the back of the shop with instructions on how to finish preparing some treatments he was working on before Breeze could put them out of business. But even in the back she couldn't focus. She sat with mortar and pestle in hand, a few dried herbs untouched in the bowl, staring at nothing while the scene in the bakery played in her mind over and over again. Emotions boiled up inside her; fear, anger, and hurt tumbled over each other with increasing intensity until Breeze knew she would explode if she didn't start moving, somewhere, anywhere. Abruptly she stood up and left the shop, the unfinished work sitting on the table behind her.

Again, her legs took over by habit. The woods behind her house swallowed her up as she started on the trail leading to the shed which she and Drake had been sharing. Hot tears rolled down her face as she thought of the joy she had found there. Growing up as an only child and watching her parent's marriage she had longed for the day when she would have someone that belonged to her and she to them. Lying at night in Drake's arms, drifting peacefully off to sleep— she felt she had found it, her special place in the world. Now it was shattered, and the pain stole her strength, her courage, and her joy.

Tears made it difficult to see and the path ahead became blurry. She was almost to the door of the shed when she realized someone else was approaching, someone tall. It was a man. Breeze blinked quickly to try to clear her vision even as she scrambled around to the back of the shed.

"Breeze, wait!"

Drake?

Drake ran up to Breeze and gathered her in his arms. The unexpected tenderness in his voice broke her resistance.

"Oh, my love," he whispered into her hair as his arms wrapped tighter around her. Part of her wanted to punch him and run but another part just wanted to be held.

"My love," he said again, "what's wrong? Where have you been? Why haven't you come to me?"

His words stopped her crying immediately. She was so confused she couldn't cry.

"What do you mean, why didn't I come?" For the second time in a week Breeze found herself wondering if she was losing her mind. "Drake, I saw you in the bakery with Elaine." She felt foolish saying something so obvious, but she didn't know what else to say.

"That's why you haven't been coming?" He seemed genuinely surprised. He cupped her face in his hands, "My beautiful girl, you know we aren't telling anyone about the marriage."

"I know we aren't telling anyone, but not telling anyone and continuing to court Elaine are two different things. I am certainly not courting Boulder."

A dark cloud flashed across Drake's gaze at the mention of Boulder but then was instantly gone. Breeze was far too confused by the current conversation to worry about such a fleeting expression.

"I have to keep up appearances or my Uncle will be suspicious. You know that my Uncle disowning me will destroy my future, *our* future. Elaine and I are intended for each other so I have to continue to act the way I did before we were married."

It struck Breeze like a shot that besides the occasional brief moment at church she had never seen Drake and Elaine spending time together. Her time was mostly consumed by her work in the shop and when she did have free time, she and Drake did not exactly move in the same circles. She felt foolish, again, for not having been more careful about the timing of her marriage to Drake, but she still didn't regret marrying him.

She laid her head against his chest. "When, when can we tell people?"

He held her close for a moment before answering. "The tournament tomorrow is a large one. If I win the joust, I will announce our marriage."

Hope soared within her, then dropped like a hawk with an arrow through its heart.

"Drake," Breeze's voice was low and serious, "do not kiss Elaine tomorrow."

"What are you talking about?"

"If the crowd demands a kiss from you and Elaine, don't do it." Breeze lifted her head from Drake's chest and stared him down as if she could shape the future by the sheer force of her will.

"Breeze, honey," Drake replied, "you know the crowds love the romance of the tournaments just as much as the violence."

"Drake, please…" Breeze was pleading now.

"What would you have me do, publicly humiliate her?" Drake countered.

Breeze hung her head and didn't respond. Drake picked up a strand of hair and tucked it behind her ear.

"You know you are the one I want to be with," Drake said, lifting her chin to kiss her forehead. She wanted to believe it. She willed herself to believe it. Drake was her dream come true. She closed her eyes, leaned into his chest, and surrendered to trust.

Chapter Thirteen

GINGER STAMPED HER hooves impatiently, snorting frozen puffs into the pre-dawn air. "Ginger!" Breeze snapped, trying desperately to fasten the cinch. "It's a two-hour ride to the tournament and if you don't stand still we'll miss the first joust." In response, Ginger repeatedly tossed her head and sidled around the stall even more. Changing tactics, Breeze grabbed the harness and stroked Ginger's soft nose. "Ginger," she crooned in her sweetest voice, "apples." Then she stared deep into the horse's eyes in what she hoped was a very meaningful way.

Whether it was the stare or the promise of apples, Ginger quieted for just a few seconds. With lightning speed, Breeze finished fastening the cinch strap. Quickly grabbing her food and bag of medical supplies, she secured them to the saddle and led Ginger out of the stall.

Once they were finally on the road, the ride through the country was beautiful, peaceful, and quiet. Breeze felt more present and calmer than she had since before she married Drake. The trees were ablaze with the colors of fall and the wet grass glimmered in the morning sun like a million tiny gems. A profound sense of gratitude settled on her heart, and she wondered if there was anything more sublime than the marriage of sunlight and morning dew. After reigning in Ginger for the first few miles to warm up her muscles, Breeze gave the restless horse her head. The countryside flew past. The beat of Ginger's hooves pounded out a rhythm in Breeze's heart. The wind caressed her face, streamed through her hair, and flew off her back, taking all her worries with it. Breeze felt free, unrestrained joy, and her heart soared.

Eventually Ginger exhausted her own spontaneous joy and, having met her need for freedom, slowed to a contented walk. Breeze decided to dismount and walk beside her. The closer they came to the city, the more Breeze's stress returned and her thoughts began to churn. Would Drake win? Would he lose? Could she handle it if he lost? Her stomach started feeling tight and a pressing weight in her forehead that made it hard to think. Maybe she didn't want to know. Maybe she should turn back. Breeze paused on the path, looking at the city ahead in the distance, columns of smoke rising into the air. Then she looked back over the dirt road and rolling hills through which she had just come. She tried to imagine how it would feel to be at home not knowing, compared to how it would be to witness the event and know for sure. The fear felt unbearable either way.

Breeze leaned for a minute against Ginger's warm, strong shoulder and took several deep breaths. Sensing her need for reassurance, Ginger stood still and waited.

"Ginger," Breeze finally said aloud, "I am going to choose to have hope that this will turn out well. I am being too pessimistic. Drake has won almost every tournament he has been in. He is a stunningly talented knight. There is no reason for me to be filled with this much fear. We are going to go to the city and we are going to watch Drake win this tournament."

Squaring her shoulders and placing hands on her hips Breeze decided to face the future with a little faith in Drake.

"Still," she said, dropping her hands and taking hold of Ginger's reins, "I think I'll walk."

Breeze remembered why she hated cities the moment she arrived. They were crowded, loud, and smelly. The bright spot in her arrival was being able to leave Ginger with Hamond, a fellow apothecary and a friend of her father's, so at least she knew her horse was well cared for. Pushing her way through the crowds, her nose and ears assaulted at every turn by the overwhelming number of smells and sounds, she made her way to the stands of the jousting arena. The moment she spotted Drake, his green and silver banner flying in the sun, her heart and stomach tried to switch places and she gave herself a stern pep talk on the uselessness of fear.

Drake was standing in a circle of knights and ladies, laughing and smiling. Breeze felt a surge of pride that this handsome, strong knight was her very own husband. She longed to go join him in the circle and take her place by his side. "Soon enough," she told herself.

The tournament began with the usual fanfare of jugglers, acrobats, and other entertainers. The crowd seemed rowdier than usual, possibly because this day was unusually cold for fall. Breeze couldn't relax either, but it had nothing to do with the weather. Everything inside was twisted in knots. Her future happiness was tied to what happened here and despite her best efforts and sternest rebukes, fear overwhelmed her. First, one set of knights came up, and then another, then another. She barely saw any of it. The cheering and booing, praises and taunts of the crowd came to her as if she were underwater. Finally, she saw Drake lining up at the head of the tilt for his first bout of the day, and immediately every detail stood out in perfect clarity.

She glanced over at the other knight and her heart sank. This man was a giant and the fierce confidence with which he held himself made Breeze feel ominous just looking at him.

Lances were lowered and the knights charged, horses gaining speed as they barreled toward each other. A loud crash sounded as the opposing knights lance made direct contact with Drake's shield. Drake's lance flew out of his hand as his torso was flattened against Balius' flanks. She watched in horror as Balius slowed to a stop near the edge of the arena and waited for his knight to move. For several long moments the arena was silent with anticipation. Then Drake rolled slowly to his side and around to a sitting position. The crowd gave their deafening approval. Drake raised his gauntleted hand and gave a little wave to show he was still in the fight.

Gathering Balius' reins, he led the war horse back around to the head of the tilt, where Aldwin handed him a fresh lance. Again, lances were lowered, and horse hooves thundered toward each other. Lances crashed and exploded. Both knights tumbled backward off their steeds. The opposing knight immediately leapt to his feet, blunted broadsword in hand, determined to win the joust, as rules allowed, by sword fight. But Drake lay motionless. Breeze began screaming at Drake as the opposing knight ducked under the tilt and rapidly closed the distance between them.

"Get up, Drake! Get up!" Her throat ached from the intensity of the scream. "Drake! Get up!"

The opposing knight lifted his sword above his head and swung downward. Drake swung his own sword straight up through the hilt of the opposing knight, knocking it out of his hands. With a lightning twist of his wrist, Drake slipped the tip of his sword between the helmet and breastplate of his opponent, stopping him short. Both knights stood frozen, Drake still seated on the ground, sword held in front of him, the opposing knight with arms out to the side, not daring to move. After a moment of stunned silence, the crowd erupted. With the slightest movement of his wrist Drake could kill the other knight, which was enough to give him the victory. Breeze felt a flood of relief and joy. Drake had won. Everyone around her leapt to their feet, cheering wildly but she remained seated, gripping the edge of her bench, staring at the ground in front of her, trying to soothe her heartbeat. Drake was one fight closer to being able to announce their marriage and she couldn't wait.

Her heart surged with pride as Drake leapt onto Balius and charged around the arena, spurring the crowd into an adoring frenzy. Then she heard it. It started slowly and quietly at first but then gained more momentum as more spectators caught on.

"Kiss! Kiss! Kiss! Kiss!"

People were stomping their feet with each chant and Breeze could feel each and every one. She looked up and saw the sight she most wanted not to see. Elaine, her perfect hair falling in a shining curtain, leaned over the wooden railing to bestow a kiss on the victorious knight, Drake McArthur. Breeze wanted to look away but her mind was frozen. As she watched their lips meet, valiant knight and beautiful lady, she knew without question that Drake was savoring every moment of the kiss. He was not simply appeasing his Uncle or pacifying the crowd. This was a kiss of pleasure, and her heart seized with pain.

Leaping up, Breeze started pushing frantically through the crowd. Her only goal was escape. She pushed and pushed through people, ignoring their angry protests at her rude behavior. Once outside the arena she started running. Each time she came to an intersection she turned down the road that seemed least crowded. Shops and people flew by in a blur as tears streamed down her face. Eventually she reached the city wall. She ran through its thick, wooden gates and kept running. She saw the forest line and headed for the safety of the trees. Branches tore at her face and clothing, but didn't slow her down. Cold seized her chest and her muscles burned. Stumbling upon a small game trail, she ran and ran. Until, all of a sudden, she fell.

Chapter Fourteen

S HE WASN'T SURE how long she fell but she knew when she hit the bottom. She lay still, paralyzed by the intensity of the pain permeating through her body and into her soul. The cold, stone floor gave nothing on impact. Her body absorbed it all. The pain slicing through her head eradicated rational thought. She blinked, but her pupils did not dilate. The blackness around her was so complete, she could not tell where it ended and she began. There was no boundary between her and it.

A moan escaped her lips but she knew she was speaking only to herself in the dark abyss of this pit when she murmured, "I hurt."

"Yes, it will do that to you."

If she had the ability, she would have been startled but as it was she could only lie still and wonder who else could possibly be down here in the deepest hole she could ever imagine. Her eyes searched uselessly in the dark for the sound of the voice. Suddenly, she saw him.

A man, dressed in linen pants, a loose green shirt with rolled-up sleeves and a brown leather vest was perched comfortably on a rock a few feet away with one leg drawn up and his arm resting on his knee. She wondered how she could see him in this intense darkness. There was no light shining from above or from his face like how she imagined an angel would be. She could simply see him. He had long steel gray hair streaked with silver which was pulled back by a leather strap at his neck. He was lean, but his sinewy forearms and calloused hands showed that he did not lack strength. Deep lines were etched around his mouth and eyes, maybe from worry or laughing or both. Beneath his strongly pronounced nose, his lips turned up softly at the corners. A keen sharpness to his eyes made her look away for fear he would know her whole story with just a moment's gaze.

"What will do that to you?" she asked, coming to herself and remembering his comment.

"The truth."

"What about the truth?"

"It will do that to you."

Either he was being deliberately cryptic or the fall had addled her brain.

"Will do what to you?" she asked, an edge of annoyance creeping into her voice.

"It will hurt you."

There was something about the knowing sound of his voice or maybe it was the unexpected gentleness in his response, but it cracked her. Like an egg that shatters from the slightest tap, all the pain came spilling out of her; the exhaustion, the confusion…the betrayal. She was embarrassed to be crying in front of this stranger, but it wasn't a choice anymore. Her body convulsed with sobs so powerful they threatened to crack a rib. At times she screamed her pain, a raw primal sound that magnified itself on the cave walls. Other times her mouth was fixed silently open in a scream only angels could hear.

Sometime during her sobbing, the man had moved closer to her. Common sense told her she should be alarmed but something deeper, something she couldn't explain, told her there was nothing to fear. When the last drop of sorrow was finally trickling out, she lay silent and exhausted. There was a stillness inside she hadn't felt in a long time. Her face was wet and slightly swollen. Small shudders shook her body at infrequent intervals.

He reached out a hand to help her up and she took it. A healing warmth immediately flowed into her body. It didn't completely eradicate the pain but it lessened it so that she could move freely again. Startled, she looked at him, questioning him with her eyes. Amused, he returned her gaze but his steady look gave nothing away.

"Who are you?" she asked softly.

"I am an old man," he responded.

"Should I call you that then? Old Man?" Breeze raised one eyebrow, a glimmer of a smile appearing on her face.

"If you like," he replied, pulling a neatly folded handkerchief out of his leather vest and handing it to her.

At first, she was afraid to touch it. It was the whitest thing she had ever seen and she was so dirty from her dash through the woods and encounter with the cave floor. But the snot and tears were drying on her face, making it stiff and uncomfortable, so she took it. The fabric had an unworldly softness, like it had come from the robe of some heavenly being. Slowly, she unfolded it and pressed it to her face with both hands just to soak in the ethereal softness of it. Once again, healing power flowed into her, smoothing the lines in her forehead and soothing her thoughts.

"What is your name?" The Old Man's voice interrupted her moment with the handkerchief.

She refused to move the fabric from her face so her reply was somewhat muffled.

"Breeze."

"Breeze? Really? Is that your real name?"

She had the vague sense he already knew the answer to that question but answered anyway.

"No."

"What is your real name?"

"I'll tell you that when you tell me yours, Old Man."

To her surprise, he chuckled.

"Fair enough," he conceded. "Why do they call you Breeze?"

"Because my Dad always says I am as pleasant as a summer breeze," she explained.

"Well, Breeze, do you know why you're here?"

What did he mean by that, she thought, immediately irritated. *I'm here because I was running blindly through the forest and fell through a hole.*

As if he sensed her thoughts he responded, "You're here because you can't fix the mess you're in."

She felt tears begin to well in her eyes again but she pushed them back down. The otherworldliness of the Old Man was no longer surprising her, so she didn't question how he knew anything about "the mess" she was in.

"The only thing you can fix," he continued, "is yourself."

"Me?!" Anger flared like fire in her chest. "I'm not the one who needs fixing! If it weren't for that lying, selfish, unfaithful beast of a knight, I wouldn't be here in the first place!"

"Whoa, Breeze," the Old Man chuckled. "Or should I call you Tempest?"

She shot him a scorching look until he took her hand in his own. There it was again. What was that? She felt the anger drain from her body through her hand, as if he were taking it from her. In its place she felt peace and reassurance.

"It's time for you to go home," he said.

Home. Her heart sank at the word. Even her hand in his couldn't stop the dread she felt at that prospect.

"But first," he said, his voice bright and cheerful, "I want to give you something." He reached into his pocket and pulled out a braided leather cord with a gold metal key on the end.

Breeze took the offered key, wondering what it opened.

"It doesn't open any physical things," the Old Man explained. "When you find yourself in a situation where you feel you have no choices or that none of them are good, you can take that key in your hand, hold it over your heart and say, "Old Man, I need you," and you will come to me, no matter where you are."

Breeze slipped the key in her pocket. She didn't believe it would do any such thing but there was no point in telling the Old Man that directly. She glanced quickly at his face to see if he read that thought, but his face revealed nothing.

She didn't want to go home, but the Old Man was right. It was time.

All around her was darkness. How would she get out of here anyway? A light with no discernable source began to glow in the cave until she could see impenetrable rock encircling all the way around.

"There is the way out," the Old Man said, gesturing towards one of the rock walls.

Breeze looked to where he was pointing and then looked dubiously back at the Old Man.

"Come," he said, "I'll show you."

Carefully, she stood to follow him, amazed that her body appeared to have very little lasting impact from the fall. As the Old Man walked toward the rock walls she noticed his gait. It was strong but not proud, humble but not apologetic. What did the way she walked say about her, she wondered?

Nearing the towering rocks, she noticed an opening she hadn't seen before. But it was black. By far the deepest darkness she had ever seen. Her steps stopped short.

"We're going that way?" she asked.

"No, I am needed elsewhere, but this is the way you will need to go if you want to get out of here."

Breeze was not one to be squeamish about the dark. At times she rather enjoyed being outside where the softness of the night air would caress her skin and her eyes would relax after the harshness of the sun. But this was no ordinary dark. This was a blackness so complete it seemed it would wrap you up and touch your soul if you dared step into it.

"Surely there is another way," Breeze said, her voice quivering.

"No. Not for you. This is your path."

She stood a moment longer, staring.

"Breeze, trust me. This is the way you need to go if you want to get home."

Lowering her eyebrows, she stared at him. "Why should I trust you?"

He shrugged. "Maybe you should. Maybe you shouldn't, but the only way you'll know is if you step into the darkness."

"It's so dark. How will I know where to go?"

"Keep walking through the darkness until you wonder if you will ever see light again. Walk a little farther and you will see the light appear. Follow the light and it will take you home."

Breeze couldn't have said why she did it. After one last glance at the solid rock walls, and then at the Old Man, she stepped into the darkness.

Chapter Fifteen

REEZE WASN'T SURE what she expected to see at the end of the dark tunnel but her heart dropped when she saw that it put her out very close to the place she fell. She noticed with some confusion that the hole she fell in was no longer there. She spotted a small wooden bridge curving over a babbling brook which tumbled happily along its way, oblivious to the cares and concerns of the human world. She decided to join it for a moment. Sitting on a rock, she listened to the water as it rushed past, carrying fall leaves tumbling down stream. Taking off her shoes, she dipped her feet in the crystal clear, cold, water.

She felt calmer than when she left the arena thanks to her visit with the Old Man, but she was still confused about how to proceed. Should she get Ginger and head home and forget she ever knew Drake McArthur? After all, no one ever blamed a river for taking the path of least resistance. Or maybe she should be brave and go back to the arena and face the situation with calm dignity? Although Drake had definitely enjoyed the kiss, she acknowledged, he hadn't initiated it. He had no control over the crowd. Should she find him and just punch him? She smiled and felt a thrill of pleasure at that thought. But no, she knew that wouldn't solve anything in the end and would just embarrass them both.

After wavering back and forth between the only two real options she had, to go back and be brave or to run away, she decided that courage was the best option. Dried leaves crunched beneath her boots as she began walking slowly back toward the arena. The farther she got from the Old Man and the closer she got to the arena, the more the pain of watching Drake savor his kiss with Elaine burrowed into her. By the time she could hear the crowd her nerves were a complete wreck. Her legs felt weak as she climbed the stairs into the stands. Thankfully, there was a spot right next to the stairs on the very bottom row.

She sank down to her seat, dropping the bag of medicines beside her, and proceeded to not watch the next hour of jousts which were happening right in front of her. She was aware enough of her surroundings to hear that Drake had already competed again and won, which made him eligible to compete in the melee, a round where six knights on horseback with swords would attempt to unseat their opponents. The last two remaining knights would joust for the grand prize. Her mind raced with a thousand different fears. Over and over again she considered running for her horse and riding home, but she was paralyzed with fear. So, when she finally saw three knights take their places at one end of the arena and three at the other, she had no choice but to watch the outcome.

The two sides barreled toward one another, the horses' covers billowing in the wind. The clash of metal when the two sides met caused the crowd to jump to its feet. Breeze could barely keep up as the knights beat each other across the arms, legs, back and head with their blunted swords. She saw one knight place the hilt of his sword in his armpit and charge an opponent who then went barreling backwards over his horse's flanks.

Sparks flew as two other knights who had broken away from the group circled each other, aggressively attacking with their swords. The yellow knight was almost imperceptibly leaning farther and farther back while his opponent leaned forward to press the advantage. Like a flash of lightning, the yellow knight shot forward, caught his opponent by the upper arm, and pulled the unbalanced knight off his horse. Four knights were left on their horses. Only two more needed to be eliminated for the final contestants to be chosen.

Drake and a purple-clad knight raced side by side down the side of the arena, clashing swords between them. Balius lashed out at the other horse which was pushing him closer and closer to the railing. As they neared the end of the curved arena, the purple knight pulled hard on the reins and threw his charger into Drake. Balius could no longer turn to take the momentum out of his forward charge and crashed sideways into the fence, shattering the wood, and crushing Drake's leg. Horse and rider screamed in pain. Seizing his advantage, the purple knight swung the flat of his sword backwards across Drake's chest and Drake crumbled to the ground.

Breeze leapt into the arena and raced down the side towards Drake, clutching her bag of medicines. It was risky and she knew it, but she had to get to Drake. As soon as she got to him she slipped her arms under his and tried to pull him under the barrier and out of the arena, but with all his armor he was dead weight. Then Lord Hadrian was there with the tournament physician.

"Drake, you fool," Lord Hadrian spat as he yanked off Drake's helmet. "Any knight with an ounce of intelligence would have seen that coming— and look what you've done to my horse." Breeze looked up and her heart ached for Balius. He was neighing and tossing his head. She noticed as he shuffled around that he was avoiding putting any weight on his front leg. She looked back at Drake, whose face was deathly pale, but Breeze could tell he was breathing and that the color of his face came from pain and not loss of blood. She and the physician worked quickly to unbuckle and untie Drake's leg armor, but as soon as it was off she wished she hadn't. What she saw made even Lord Hadrian turn away for a moment.

"Foolish boy!" he exclaimed, holding a white handkerchief to his nose. "What good are you as a knight with a leg like that?"

Drake's lower leg had snapped completely, his shin bone protruding from the skin.

"Lord Hadrian, I recommend we amputate his leg so as to prevent infection. It is too mutilated and simply can't be fixed," the physician stated as if discussing the weather at afternoon tea.

"No!" Breeze shouted. "Please don't," she pleaded. While the physician was speaking she had already yanked open her bag and began treating the wound. She mashed yarrow leaves with water from a flask, then packed the poultice into the wound to stop the bleeding. As she spoke she yanked out a bandage to begin wrapping the wound. "My dad can fix this. I know he can. I've seen him do it. This is a clean break and can be reset. Please, Lord Hadrian."

Lord Hadrian looked back and forth from skilled, respected physician to young girl.

While he was debating, Elaine came rushing up to their small group. She fell on her knees near Drake and began stroking his hair and face. "Oh, my sweet love," she cried. Drake moaned and turned his head but said nothing.

Breeze wanted to break down and weep. This whole day had been too much and to witness Elaine's tender affection for Drake in an already tense moment nearly broke her. But she knew that possibly Drake's life and certainly his happiness were in her hands right now. So instead she quickly threw a part of her skirt over the wounded part of Drake's leg. The bandage she had applied couldn't quite cover the grotesque nature of the injury and she didn't need Elaine fainting or vomiting right now.

"Please," Breeze tried again when she saw that Lord Hadrian still hadn't made up his mind. "I have some dwale. It will sedate him for the journey and allow my father to fix his leg. Lord Hadrian, you know Drake. If he survives the amputation he will most likely kill himself when he finds himself a cripple. He won't want to live if he can't be a knight."

She could tell by the look on Lord Hadrian's face that she had struck a chord.

"I don't want him to live if he's a cripple," he snapped. "The fool will be on my hands forever. You can take his sorry carcass and do what you want with it. If your father can't fix his leg we will cut it off and then he can do us all a favor and kill himself if he wants."

"I can bring him to you in my carriage," Elaine offered.

"Thank you, Elaine, that is most helpful. I will give him some dwale so he won't feel a thing. Do not go gently, but come with all haste. The sun will set on us before we complete our journey if you do not."

Lord Hadrian turned to some knights who had been eliminated earlier. "You there! Come carry this knight to this lady's carriage."

Breeze quickly poured a few spoonfuls of dwale into Drake's mouth before he was carried away. She wanted to say something to him, to comfort him as Elaine had done but knew she couldn't. She cursed again the circumstances that forced them to keep their marriage a secret, but there was not time to dwell on that now.

Shoving her supplies back in her bag, Breeze jumped up and raced off to gather Ginger. As soon as she saw her horse, she flung her arms around Ginger's neck and pressed her cheek against the warm fur. Then she quickly saddled Ginger and raced off. It took everything she had to occasionally reign Ginger in to catch her breath. She knew Ginger would permanently damage herself trying to travel as fast as Breeze wanted if Breeze asked it of her. On the way home Breeze noticed nothing. The only thing she could think of was getting Drake to her father.

Chapter Sixteen

THE MOMENT SHE reached home she leapt off Ginger and raced inside. Dark was falling and she silently prayed Elaine would get there quickly.

"Dad! Dad! Get the comfrey! Grab the box, splints and linens!"

Breeze was frantically rushing around the shop gathering the necessary supplies. Both parents came rushing into the shop from where they had been relaxing by the fire.

"Breeze, what is going on?" her dad asked, one hand on his hip and the other grasping his hair.

"Drake broke his leg at the tournament. Elaine is bringing him in the carriage. I need you to fix it. Mom, will you please see to Ginger. I rode her hard and then left her outside."

Without a word, her mom walked out the back door.

"Why didn't you take him to Hamond instead of bringing the poor boy all the way back here?"

Breeze paused from her frantic rummaging and looked into her dad's eyes.

"It's not that kind of break, Dad. Hamond can't do it."

Galen's lips set in a grim line. "I see."

Breeze went back to her frantic rummaging. "Where are the suturing needles and the catgut?"

Her father laid a calming hand on her back. "Fear has never helped us."

Seeing his gentleness and quiet confidence weakened all the strong defenses Breeze had thrown up to deal with this situation. Tears escaped her eyes and began rolling down her cheeks.

Galen's brows pulled down in a pensive frown. "What does this boy mean to you?"

"Nothing," she lied. "I'm just tired."

"Well, dry your tears and clear your mind. I hear the carriage."

Breeze welcomed the numbness of heart that she needed to focus on her task. Elaine's driver and Galen carried Drake inside and laid him on the table which Breeze had hastily cleared. Breeze noticed that Elaine had removed the rest of Drake's armor and she found herself praising Elaine for her good thinking.

Drake moaned in pain as they laid him on the table.

"How much dwale did you give him?" Galen asked.

"Not enough to get him through the bone setting," she responded.

"Give him some more."

Breeze obeyed and poured a few more spoonfuls into Drake's mouth.

"Elaine, I will need you to come stand at Drake's head just in case he wakes up," Galen commanded. "Wrap your arms around his chest and hold tight. Also, tell me if you notice any problems with his breathing. Too little dwale and he will wake up too soon—too much and he will never wake up at all. Breeze, come hold his foot still."

Galen began unwrapping the bandage covering the wound. Breeze glanced over at Elaine to check her reaction. She was sitting on a low stool, her arms around Drake's chest and her cheek pressed to his. To her surprise, Elaine neither fainted or vomited. She merely turned a little pale and continued to hold onto Drake. Breeze would have felt better if Elaine had shown some sign of weakness, had given Breeze some reason to look down on her, but she didn't. *She's never anything less than perfect*, Breeze thought, feeling small and worthless.

Her dad's words interrupted her thoughts. "Well done with the yarrow leaves. I will clean those out and then try to massage this bone back into place. I can't tell if there is any internal bleeding but if there is you need to understand that he may still lose the leg."

Breeze and Elaine looked at each other, pain registering on both faces. Elaine's brows pulled together as if a thought was beginning to occur to her. Breeze immediately looked away, worried that in intervening for Drake she had betrayed them both.

"The good thing is," her dad continued, "it barely broke the surface and it's a clean break. So, let's see what we can do."

The room fell into a tense silence as Galen began the slow process of cleaning the wound and then gently pushing the bone back into place. Breeze was amazed by how slowly and methodically he worked. Some of the pushes he made on the bone moved it an imperceptible amount, but as the time passed Breeze could tell the bone was slowly moving back into place. She admired his patience. It was one of his skills as an apothecary that she knew she lacked. He had the patience to let plants grow, medicines steep, and wounds heal. He understood that sometimes the best cures were not always the quickest.

Breeze reflected on her current situation with Drake. She wondered how her life would be different now if she possessed a little more of her father's careful patience.

"The linens are soaking in the bowl of comfrey and hot water. Bring those to me please. Also grab the splints and felt."

When Breeze brought the supplies, her father said, "I'm going to wash this blood off my hands. Can you finish here?"

Breeze nodded silently. She wrapped the wet bandages around Drake's leg. Then she laid felt over the bandages and finished by wrapping wooden splints around his leg. Galen came over with what looked like an unfinished rectangular box that was open on the top and sides. They worked together to put Drake's leg inside and wrap linen around the box to hold his leg.

"What happens now?" Elaine asked.

Breeze realized that it was the first time she had spoken since coming into the shop.

"He will stay here for the night," her father responded. "In the morning we will return him to the castle. We will watch him for signs of infection or internal bleeding. If all goes well, in about 12 days we will be able to put a plaster on the leg which he will wear for 8 to 10 weeks. After that he should be able to walk again."

Elaine spontaneously threw her arms around Galen's neck and then just as quickly let go.

"Thank you," she said quietly.

"Please do not thank me yet," Galen replied. "There are no guarantees with this sort of thing. Drake is not safe yet."

Elaine simply nodded her head and left with her driver.

Galen turned to Breeze. "I imagine you are exhausted from such a long day. Why don't you go to bed and I will stay up with our patient."

Breeze shook her head. "I would like to stay up with him."

Galen looked searchingly into his daughter's eyes. "Breeze," he began but she cut him off.

"Dad, I can't."

He said nothing more but continued to look into her eyes. Knowing she caused the hurt she saw there made her want to crawl into a hole and hide. He knew now that she was hiding something from him.

After a moment he turned to leave the room but paused at the doorway and said, "Stay vigilant. When Drake wakes he may try to get off the table and that could undo what we have done."

"Thank you, Dad. I will."

With her father gone, Breeze sank into the chair that Elaine had left.

She wanted to kiss Drake's face, to press her cheek to his as Elaine had done, but she knew she had already done enough to jeopardize their secret.

Their secret.

She was beginning to believe the weight of it would kill her. Then she thought of the Old Man. She remembered him telling her she couldn't fix the mess she was in, and that was before Drake broke his leg. Now their future together was even more uncertain. Tears rolled down her cheeks. She also remembered the healing warmth that had flowed through her body when he took her hand. She wished he was here now. Maybe he could heal Drake. Maybe he could make everything better and all her problems go away. With that thought she let out a long breath, looked up at the ceiling and let the long night of waiting begin.

"Breeze…Breeze…Breeze, where are we?"

Breeze lifted her head off the table, squinting at the morning sunlight streaming through the open door and then looked at Drake whose pale face was just a few inches away. He moaned, and his breath smelled like dwale. She recoiled at the stench, then answered. "You had an accident yesterday during the melee. You broke your leg and my dad fixed it." She brushed a strand of hair from his forehead and bent down to kiss it.

Just then her father came in and she sat bolt upright.

"Good morning, Drake. How is the patient?"

"I don't know. My leg hurts," Drake said slowly, sounding confused.

"Well, if it weren't for the young lady here it would hurt a lot worse. The tournament physician wanted to amputate your lower leg but Breeze convinced them to let her bring you to me and we were able to put you back together."

The grateful way Drake looked at her fed her soul like the sun feeds a flower.

"It was actually Elaine who brought you here in her carriage. I couldn't have done it without her."

"Where's Balius?"

Breeze shifted uncomfortably. "Balius was hurt. I don't know where he is."

Galen heard the shop to the door open and left to check on their first customer.

"Breeze, come around where I can see you," Drake commanded weakly. When she had done so he took her hand and held it. "Is it true they were going to amputate my leg and you saved it?"

"It's not saved yet," Breeze countered, "but yes, they wanted to amputate your leg."

"Thank you." The sincerity in his voice caused a rush of love for this kind, beautiful man, her husband.

As much as she didn't want to Breeze said, "We need to get you back to the castle. I will notify Lord Hadrian, and he can send someone for you."

"No," Drake said sharply and then again more softly, "No. I will manage."

Breeze gave Drake a concerned frown. From her minimal interactions with Lord Hadrian she was beginning to realize there was more to Drake's relationship with his uncle than she currently understood.

"Let me go fetch Boulder then. He and his father can easily get you back to the castle."

"No," Drake snapped, but this time there was no following softness.

Breeze's own irritation was beginning to rise. "Why? It's not like he's going to drop you. Boulder could probably lift a small horse. He would definitely not struggle with you."

"I am not going to let that overgrown beast of burden touch me. I said no. Go fetch Aldwin. He will get me home."

"Aldwin! He is half Boulder's size! Drake, that's ridiculous. You have to protect your leg. Our future depends on it! Aldwin won't be able to help you out the door much less up the hill."

The look on Drake's face changed in an instant from irritation to the loving gratitude she had seen earlier. He grabbed her hand again.

"Thank you," he whispered and she could see small tears in the corner of his eyes.

He pulled her down and kissed her. She savored the kiss for just a moment then pulled back laughing.

"You taste like dwale, and that is quite possibly the grossest kiss I've ever had."

He laughed as well but stopped short when he saw Elaine enter the room. Seeing the look on his face Breeze spun around as well.

"I've just been talking to Galen in the front room and he says you are ready to go," she said to Drake. "He explained everything to me about what we can expect as you heal."

The way Elaine used the word "we" struck Breeze like a fist to the chest. At the same time her heart pounded with fear. Had she seen or heard anything? She didn't appear to have but that was no guarantee.

Galen entered the back room, rescuing the secret lovers from the need to respond.

"Good news, Drake. Elaine is here to take you to the castle. The driver and I will get you loaded now.

"Thank you, Galen."

Galen stared silently at Drake for the briefest of moments, trying to see into what this boy meant to his daughter, then simply responded, "You're welcome." Turning to Breeze he instructed, "Why don't you go upstairs and lie down. You've worked and sacrificed enough for one day."

With a last look at Drake, Breeze began to climb the stairs to her room. She could hear the bustle downstairs as Drake was moved to Elaine's carriage. She removed her shoes and dress, washed her hands and face from a small bowl of water next to her bed, then laid down, and wept. All the stress and fear and work came bubbling up and pouring out and she let it come and let it go.

Chapter Seventeen

THE NEXT DAY as twilight settled in, Breeze slung her medicine bag over her shoulder and head up the hill to the castle to check on Drake. Aldwin was waiting for her by the front gate and led her to a small drawing room. Drake was slouched into a window seat, staring out at the darkening sky, with his injured leg propped up in front of him and his other foot absently pushing on the head of a bear rug whose jaws were open in a forever silent ferocious roar. Breeze noticed with concern that Drake's hair was uncombed, his shirt untucked and his pants un-pressed.

A dying fire explained why the room was so chilly. Breeze hurried over to stoke the fire and add a few logs, bringing the fire back to life.

When he still hadn't noticed her she asked, "How is the invalid?"

The moment he saw her his face beamed, his smile lighting up her heart like the morning sun.

"Breeze!" he exclaimed, starting to get up but Breeze quickly stopped him.

"No, sit. I'll come to you." She moved towards his leg but he grabbed her hand and pulled her onto his lap.

"How's my little savior doing?"

"It wasn't just me," she deflected, demurely lowering her head.

"Well, no one else's talents would have mattered if you hadn't stood up to my uncle— which, let's be honest, is something I won't even do."

"Speaking of talent, I really must look at your leg. It's what I came to do."

"Really?" he asked, playfully arching an eyebrow. "I thought you came because you missed me as much as I missed you."

"Well, I do miss you. So much that I want your leg to get better so you can win all your tournaments, announce our marriage, and I will never have to leave you again."

"Sounds like heaven," he said, leaning back against the stone wall.

"If by heaven you mean that it's something you've heard about but never experienced then yes, being openly married to Drake McArthur sounds exactly like heaven. Now let me look at your leg."

While Breeze worked on rebandaging the leg with a new comfrey poultice, she and Drake chatted easily about news at the castle, work, and the other ins and outs of life. Breeze began working slowly as she neared the end of her task but knew she couldn't drag it out forever. When she finally finished and the new bandage had been applied, Breeze stood to go but Drake grabbed her hand and looked longingly into her eyes.

"Come again tomorrow?" he asked.

"Unfortunately, your leg doesn't require that much attention, but I will come back in a few days when the swelling has gone down to put on the plaster cast."

The thought of going home put a knot in Breeze's stomach. The power of keen observation and an almost mystical level of intuition combined to make Galen the highly successful apothecary that he was. Unfortunately, both powers were in full force when Breeze brought Drake to the shop. Refusing to discuss anything with her father had put an almost unbearable strain on their relationship. The silence between them had become like the fourth member of their family.

A week later, as she was gathering supplies to head to the castle, her father came and laid a hand on her shoulder. He held her gaze for a moment and Breeze almost broke at the pain she saw there. It surprised her to realize how long it had been since she last looked deeply at her father, or anyone for that matter. From a young age, her father taught her to always look in to people's eyes. It was the first source of information for how they are feeling, he would say.

"I just need you to know," Galen said, "that if you ever need anything, I am here for you." And then he walked away. Hastily shoving the rest of the supplies into the bag, Breeze rushed out the door before the tears could fall.

She wanted to get to the castle as soon as possible so Drake could wrap his arms around her and comfort her, but the moment she stepped into the drawing room she could sense his mood was darker than before.

"I'm here to put on your cast," Breeze said tentatively.

Drake made a distracted sound of assent but kept staring out the tall arched window, barely acknowledging her presence.

Without speaking she sat next to Drake's leg and began laying out the resin, wax and linens she needed to form the cast.

"Because of your injury we have had to keep our marriage a secret a lot longer than expected."

Drake stared stonily out the window.

She wanted to just come out and say what she wanted, to tell her parents about the marriage, but fear of his reaction made her mind spin like a wheel in slick mud. Breeze took a deep breath, and told herself to just open her mouth and say it, but her words were stuck.

Drake broke the silence. "Are you almost done?"

The simple sentence hurt Breeze. This wasn't how their last visit had gone.

"Yes, but I—"

"That's good. I'm tired today. I will need you to leave as soon as you're done."

"Of course, but Drake I…"

He stared straight at her now but his expression was void of emotion. "What?" he snapped.

She wanted to just drop the conversation and leave but she knew she wouldn't see him again for several days, if not weeks, and she couldn't bear the pain of the keeping a secret from her parents any longer.

"I want to tell my parents about our marriage. I know they won't tell anyone else. My dad knows something is going on and it is hurting me to keep this secret from him."

"No."

And that was it. No understanding. No discussion. Just no. Breeze felt like a child who had been dismissed by a parent. She couldn't give up that easily though. This was too important to her. She tried again.

"My parents are good people, maybe they can help—"

"No."

There it was again. Drake was not even acknowledging her presence now. He was looking out the window, his mind far away.

Breeze finished forming the cast, wiped her hands, gathered her materials and left without saying another word. There was nothing to say.

When she got home she walked silently past her father and up the stairs to her room. She felt ill. Not physically, but her heart, her mind—they were tired. Tired from secrets, tired from yearning, tired of the wild ups and downs that started the moment she saw Drake in the shop.

As she lay down on the bed she remembered something the Old Man had said to her. *"When you find yourself in a situation where you feel you have no choices or that none of them are good…"*

She wondered for a moment if she still had the key. She jumped off her bed, slightly panicked, ready to search high and low until she found it but there it was, laying in plain sight on top of her dresser. *That's odd*, she thought. *I don't remember putting that there.* But she picked up the golden key, held it to her heart and said, "Old Man, I need you."

Chapter Eighteen

$\mathcal{S}$HE WAS STANDING on a dirt path in a desert landscape. Heat poured over her. Sagebrush, cactus, and other desert plants stretched on and on in a vast open landscape to her right. To her left, the path wound up a steep cliff. Without any particular reason, she decided to go up. She climbed until her legs burned and sweat poured down her back. "Old Man!" she called out. Nothing. She climbed, eyes searching everywhere as the sweat trickled down her scalp and into her eyes. "Old Man!" She called his name every couple minutes between ragged breaths until it began to sound more like a screech than a yell.

The longer she climbed, the angrier she became. *Irritating Old Man. He gives me a worthless key and promises to help me and instead here I am wandering around some scorching desert all by myself.*

"You know what, Old Man?" Breeze screamed into the air. She yanked the key from around her neck and hurled it off the cliff. "You can keep your useless key! I don't need you anyway! I need someone who can actually be there for me! Not some *traitor* who is going to abandon me in the middle of a godforsaken desert!"

"Hello, Tempest." He appeared out of nowhere holding the key Breeze had just defiantly thrown away. If he heard any of what she had just said, he didn't show it. Seeing him standing so calmly deflated her anger until she felt small and tired. "What's brought you here?" he asked.

"Drake won't let me tell my parents about the marriage."

"That's an interesting choice of words."

"What do you mean?"

"Well, is Drake holding you down with his hand over your mouth?"

"No," Breeze snapped.

"Then, why can't you tell your parents about the marriage?"

"You know the answer to that," Breeze responded sullenly.

"Do I?" the Old Man replied, looking surprised.

"Drake doesn't want me to."

"And?"

"And…what?"

"You want to tell your parents about the marriage and Drake doesn't want to tell your parents. Explain to me why Drake gets what he wants— just because he wants it?"

Breeze stared at the Old Man. She felt a shift inside her mind that left her feeling a little confused. She made a half-hearted attempt to defend Drake.

"He has his reasons. If his uncle finds out about the marriage he will cut Drake off. He needs to earn enough to support us before he can tell anyone. Without his uncle he has no armor, no horse, no home. Nothing."

"Seems to me like something he should have thought of before he took you as his wife."

Breeze didn't even try to respond.

"What about your father?" the Old Man asked. "He does well enough in his business, does he not? Could he help?"

At the mention of her father, her chest tightened and her throat clenched.

"He will not be happy. He did not support my relationship with Drake and will be disappointed at what I have done…" Her voice died off as she tried to regain control of her emotions. "But he will not turn us out."

"Seems to me like you have options then. From what I understand you have your father's talent and have worked hard to obtain his skill. Could Drake not support you in your work as an apothecary?"

Breeze looked at the Old Man like he had started speaking a foreign language. The concept he was presenting was almost impossible for her mind to process in its current frame.

"Drake would never want to do that," Breeze said slowly, her mind still trying to comprehend his suggestion.

"Ah. We are back to what Drake wants."

The Old Man could tell Breeze was trying to understand their conversation so he waited for a few moments before he asked, "What did Drake say when you told him you would like to tell your parents?"

"He said, no."

"And…"

"And what? He just said no."

"Did he make any comments that showed that he understood and recognized your point of view or did he ask any questions to show that he was at least trying to understand?"

Breeze looked at the Old Man blankly. She answered slowly, quietly, all while looking sideways at the Old Man.

"No."

"Will you be able to be content in a marriage where you are silenced?"

Breeze wanted to immediately answer that of course she wanted to have a voice in her relationship. She wanted to confidently state that she would never let anyone silence her or treat her like a child. But the truth was much harder to bear. She did allow Drake to silence her. He did treat her like a child and she accepted it.

She didn't like the way this new realization made her feel. She felt betrayed, but not by Drake…by herself.

They sat for a few moments in silence, the Old Man absently running his finger through the dirt while Breeze sat unmoving, brows pulled together in a pensive frown.

The Old Man broke the silence. "Are you thirsty?"

"What?"

The Old Man asked again, pronouncing each word slowly and clearly but without sarcasm, "Are you thirsty?"

Breeze had been so consumed with her thoughts she hadn't noticed how extremely thirsty she was.

"Yes, very."

Unstopping the top to the leather flask slung round his shoulders, he paused. "This water comes from the Eternal Spring and is the best water you will ever taste." Without warning he tipped the leather pouch over and poured the water onto the dry, dusty earth at Breeze's feet.

Breeze was instantly angry.

"What are you doing?" she demanded. "You never make any sense! You offer me water and then you waste it!" The parched feeling of her mouth and throat served to fuel her indignation. "What good is it to me on the ground?"

The Old Man didn't answer her but reached into his coat and pulled out a small wooden cup which he held out for her. She snatched it rudely from his hand but he didn't flinch. For a moment she actually considered not holding out the cup just to be spiteful, but her growing thirst prevented her prideful petulance. Reluctantly, she thrust the cup toward him.

A small grin played around one corner of his mouth and he poured water into the cup. Breeze lifted the water to her mouth and drank. He was right. It was the sweetest, smoothest water she had ever tasted. She could feel it nourishing her body as it flowed into her.

When she had drained the cup and lowered it from her mouth, the Old Man wrapped his hands around hers and the cup.

"Love is the water. Boundaries are the cup. Without boundaries, love is too soon spent and wasted. Boundaries hold love like the cup holds water so that it can be cherished and savored for a long, long time."

"What is a boundary?"

"Boundaries are limits that protect our safety and serenity."

"I did try to set a boundary with Drake once. I told him not to kiss Elaine and he did it anyway. So what good was that boundary to me?"

"Boundaries are limits that we place on ourselves. You can set boundaries about your time, your emotional resources, your physical space, how and when you will communicate with others or anything you need for safety or serenity, but boundaries do not tell another person what to do. Boundaries tell the other person what you are going to do given a certain set of circumstances."

Breeze stared blankly at the Old Man so he continued. "For example, you could tell Drake, if you kiss Elaine again, I will not kiss you. That would be a boundary. You are telling Drake what you will do if he does not honor your need for physical loyalty."

Breeze was still confused. "What boundary am I supposed to set with Drake?"

"That's for you to decide. But you'll know you have set the right boundary when the fear, anger, and resentment start to fade."

The next breath she was back in her room, standing next to her table, clutching the key in her hand. She could still feel the perspiration on her forehead and taste the cool water in her mouth. Absently, she placed the key on the table and walked downstairs.

She felt confused by the things the Old Man had said about love and boundaries. She felt sure her parents loved each other. Did they ever set boundaries? She had never noticed. She knew there was very little conflict in their marriage. Unlike many of her friends, she had never seen her parents raise their voices to each other. But was there limited conflict in their marriage because they had no boundaries or because they respected each other's boundaries?

Breeze wandered into the kitchen and sat down at the table. A memory came to her of a time that Caroline was visiting right before a meal. Breeze's mother announced the meal was ready. Then she waited for about five minutes. Breeze arrived for the meal but she could hear her father still moving around in the back room. Breeze, Caroline and her mother sat down and began to eat without her father, Caroline shifting uncomfortably in her seat the whole time. Later, when she and Breeze were alone she asked, "Doesn't your mother wait for your father before she eats?"

Breeze explained that the last time she remembered her mother waiting for her father at a meal time was when she was very small. Darla had told Galen, who had a hard time leaving his work, several times that the meal was ready. After many gentle and then increasingly firm reminders to come to the table, her father finally showed up, over an hour after the meal was prepared when all the food was cold. Her mother was furious. She walked away from the table, her food untouched, and didn't return for the rest of the night. That was the last time she remembered her mother waiting for her father. Ever since then she has put the meal on the table, announced it, waited about five minutes and then sat down to peacefully enjoy her meal while the food was still hot—whether anyone had joined her or not.

So what boundary could she set with Drake? As Breeze thought about it she realized that she wanted to tell her parents about the marriage but even more than that she never wanted to be dismissed like a child in a conversation again. Her finger traced patterns of the grain in the table as she tried to understand her own heart and how she would communicate her boundary to Drake.

Breeze stood up and began pacing back and forth in front of the table muttering to herself as she practiced what she would say.

"Drake, you can't...no, the Old Man said a boundary doesn't tell someone what to do...Drake, I need you to...oh, have mercy, that's still telling him what to do...this is ridiculous...Drake, in the future, if I bring up a concern or make a request and you dismiss me without even trying to understand my point of view or meet me my need, then I will not allow you to dictate my actions." That was it.

She blew out her breath, which she didn't realize she had been holding, put her hands on her hips and squared her shoulders. She could do this. Then the fear set in. A fist grabbed her chest and began to squeeze. What if he got really angry? What if he decided she wasn't worth staying with if she set a boundary? What if she ruined everything? Clutching her elbows and hunching her shoulders, her pacing resumed with more energy, her steps falling hard on the wooden floor. Maybe she should just let it go. It probably wasn't worth it. She would just do what she needed to do to keep the peace so she could keep Drake in her life because that was the most important thing. He was the most important thing.

Then she heard the Old Man's voice inside her head, haunting her, *"Will you be able to be content in a marriage where you are silenced?"*

Breeze stopped. She placed her hands on her hips again and flexed her shoulders backwards, trying to make the fist in her chest let go. She took a deep breath in through her nose and then slowly out through pursed lips. It was time to talk to Drake.

Chapter Nineteen

T HE SOFT CARESS of fall gave way to the iron grip of winter and everything turned hard. The dirt in Breeze's beloved garden, so soft and rich in the spring, turned into a solid, frozen mass from which no life could form. The cold also froze Breeze's courage. As soon as he could manage a hobble, Drake began sending her notes to meet him again at the shed, and she complied. The experience in the drawing room had been unsettling. She didn't know why his mood had so drastically changed, nor why it had changed back when he sent for her. She felt fearful and eager to please, so she hid the boundary in her heart and carried the strain of her secret alone.

Eventually, it was time for the cast to come off and Breeze decided this would be the day. She was going to set her boundary.

"Boundaries are the cup. They hold the love. Boundaries are the cup. Love is the water. Boundaries are the cup. They hold the love," Breeze muttered to herself as she walked down the street and started up the hill to the castle. There was still a fist in her chest but she walked with a determined stride. Head down, she marched on repeating the mantra, "Boundaries are the cup. They hold the love."

The way to the drawing room was now a familiar route and Breeze nodded politely to the castle servants as they passed each other in the hallway. Pausing outside the big, wooden doors, she smoothed her dress and used her hands to check her hair. She had taken extra care to look nice this morning, hoping it would help the conversation with Drake go more smoothly. She had noticed in the past that he was more likely to listen to her and treat her with respect when she looked nice.

"Good day, Drake," she greeted him, as she walked in.

He immediately beamed a smile at her and Breeze let out an audible sigh of relief that he was in a good mood. She noticed that his hair was neatly combed and pulled back, his white linen shirt was clean and tucked in to his black pants, and he was wearing a brown leater boot on his good leg. Knowing that she wanted to speak privately with him she pushed the heavy doors closed behind her.

"There's my guardian angel and my reason for living. Come, sit down next to me," Drake said, patting the space next to him in the window seat.

Drake's praise made Breeze glow with warmth.

"I saved your leg, not your life," she replied with a smile.

"One in the same, my love. If I can't be a knight, I don't want to even draw breath."

He pulled her close and began kissing her. It felt warm and wonderful in his arms. She considered just letting it all go. She was probably overreacting. Who knew if he would ever do it again, anyway. This moment was so wonderful and she didn't want to ruin it. Then she remembered the Old Man's words again, *"Will you be able to be content in a relationship where you are silenced?"* Then she heard the Old Man's voice in her mind again, but this time he was saying something new. *"If he loves you, he won't be angry."*

The words struck Breeze with their veracity. She knew then that she didn't need to be so afraid of having this conversation. Drake loved her. He would understand.

She broke the kiss and pushed Drake gently away.

"What's wrong, love. Don't you like it?"

"Of course, I like it. I love it, but we need to talk."

"Of course," Drake responded, stroking her hair.

Breeze wanted so badly to open her mouth and speak but she couldn't. It's like the words were frozen inside her. Instead she distracted herself by laying out her tools and beginning to cut through the cast. They sat in silence while she worked. Drake seemed content to let her take her time with whatever she needed to say. As she reached the end of the cast she knew she had to speak up now or she never would. She hurriedly wiped his leg and pulled down his pants leg. Standing, she also pulled him to his feet.

"Try putting your weight on it," she instructed.

Drake tentatively put weight on the freed leg and a smile spread across his face.

"It feels great!" he exclaimed. "A little weak but that can be fixed with practice."

Breeze launched in. "When I told you about wanting to tell my parents about the marriage you told me no and wouldn't discuss it with me. It made me feel like a child. That you wouldn't even discuss it with me or listen to my reasons made me feel like I had no voice. In the future, I will agree to do, or not do, only those things which we discuss and agree on together."

She did it! She set a boundary, and it felt great!

"My love," Drake said, leaning in to kiss her forehead. "We didn't discuss it because there is nothing to discuss. I did listen. We simply can't tell your parents so there is nothing to talk about."

"I don't understand why we can't tell my parents," Breeze responded, her confidence wavering.

Drake smiled down at her, "One thing I love about you is your naïve innocence. The more people we tell the higher the risk the secret will get out and the consequences will be too great. It's not worth the risk."

Breeze was starting to feel confused. He sounded so logical and confident. She was beginning to feel that maybe she was wrong after all.

She decided to try one more time. "Winning tournaments isn't the only option. We could find other ways to make a living."

"So, you want me to give up my dreams? You want me to make pittance shoveling horse manure and watch our children starve?" She could hear hardness creeping into his voice.

Her heart dropped.

"No, that's not what I said, I—"

"Yes, that is what you said. You want me to give up my dreams of being a knight just so you can tell your parents. You want to break our agreement. When we got married we agreed that we would keep our marriage a secret until I could earn a living for us. Now you are trying to change it."

"We didn't know you would get injured when we got married," she pleaded.

"So, you are just going to give up on me? Just like that? One little bump in the road and you abandon your promises?" Each sentence fell like a hammer blow on her heart.

"No, Drake, I won't—" Breeze felt frantic and confused, like the world was spinning and she couldn't make sense of it.

"Yes, Breeze, you are," Drake said emphatically, his anger rising. "How can you be so selfish? I have done nothing but love you, even though it means I could lose everything. Are you trying to ruin my future? Is that it? You want to just go tell the whole world about us so I can lose my Uncle's support, be labeled as unchivalrous and never be able to compete again? You will ruin me!"

"Stop it!" Breeze screamed. "I didn't say that! I don't want to tell the whole world. I just want to tell my parents."

"Which is like telling the whole world!" Drake countered. "Why do we need to tell anyone? It's no one else's business. You're wrong if you think your parents are going to keep a secret like that. Your busybody dad is going to be blabbing it to every sick person who comes stumbling into his pitiful shop."

"Stop it," her voice cracked, lowering to a defeated whisper. "Why are you being so mean?"

Confusion threatened to overwhelm Breeze as she struggled to remember how this conversation had even started.

"I just want us to talk about it," she tried again but her words felt like a wounded animal struggling to crawl to safety. "I want to feel like you are at least willing to listen to me."

"You are the one who isn't listening to me. I told you from the beginning that I didn't want to tell anyone until our future was secure."

"Things have changed, Drake," Breeze pleaded.

"No, Breeze," Drake responded. "You've changed."

He contemplated her then with so much contempt it felt like a physical force. "I regret it," he spat. "I regret marrying you. You weren't worth ruining my life for."

And just like that, the light inside of Breeze went out. Only pain and darkness remained.

"You need to get out," Drake said. He grabbed her by the arm as he hobbled to the door. Opening the door, he shoved her into the hallway, and closed the door in her face.

Breeze felt trapped in this public place. She felt too weak to move but she couldn't just fall apart right there in the hallway. She summoned up an image of her father's face, the one he always used when he didn't want the patient, or anyone else, to know how desperate a situation really was. She could do this. She turned her face to stone. She turned her heart to stone. She shoved down everything that had just happened so that she could walk out of the castle without making a scene. Her heart was bleeding to death, but her face said she was fine. It was the skill of an apothecary, and in this moment, she mastered it.

When she finally reached the safety of her bedroom, she grabbed the key, collapsed on her bed and cried, "Old Man, I need you.

Chapter Twenty

THIS TIME BREEZE found herself in a forest next to a cool, mountain stream. She could tell it hadn't rained in a few weeks because of the muddy banks. The Old Man was sitting quietly next to the stream, watching the water flow.

"You were wrong!" she yelled as soon as she saw him, her voice choking on her words. "You said that a boundary would hold the love that Drake has for me but it didn't. You lied! He wishes we'd never gotten married."

"Did I?" The Old Man was calm like always, and it infuriated Breeze. "I said that boundaries hold the love, but I didn't say who it would hold the love for."

"What are you talking about? I hate it when are so cryptic." Breeze clenched her fists in frustration.

"What about you, Breeze? What about the love you feel for yourself?"

"Why do I need to love myself?" Breeze asked, her anger draining from sheer exhaustion. "Father Paul teaches that we need to love others, not ourselves." Then, remembering Drake's scathing words, she asked, "What if I really am as worthless as he makes me feel?" Her voice was barely audible, almost as if her wounded words lacked the strength to make themselves heard.

Splat!

Her face was suddenly covered in dark, sticky, smelly mud. It seemed to have penetrated every part of her face in an instant, even making it into her nose and ears. She wiped her eyes and looked up to see the Old Man, his right hand still dripping from the muck.

Normally Breeze would have been livid, but her soul was too weak.

"Why did you do that?" she choked out, her voice breaking with hurt and betrayal.

In response, he silently leaned down and scooped up another handful of mud and lifted his arm. This time her rage erupted.

"No!" Her hand shot out and grabbed his wrist in a vice-like grip. She jerked his hand sharply, making the mud fall to the ground. Her eyes bored into his while her steely voice commanded, "Don't."

The Old Man brought his other hand up and pressed it firmly on hers.

"Exactly, Breeze. Yes," he whispered fiercely. His eyes bored back into hers, locking her in. Two tears held their place at the corners of his eyes. He lifted his free hand from hers and placed it on her muddy cheek.

"Never," he said in a voice that left her unsure if he was pleading or commanding. "Never let another person tell you who you are. You—" he paused while the tears let go and freely fell. "You are exquisite, and there is no human qualified for the task."

Breeze could feel her throat tighten. One brave tear left her own eye and began its muddy descent down her cheek, clearing away as much filth as it could.

"You are not a blank slate for any passerby with a dirty quill to spread his ink upon. Your soul was written by the stars. Both the glory of heaven and the humility of earth exist inside you. You cannot be rewritten."

Breeze felt something indescribably powerful inside as he spoke, but she also felt that the words he was speaking could not possibly be true of her.

He knew. She could see it in his eyes. He knew she was struggling to believe what he said.

"Come," said the Old Man. "Let's get you washed off."

The Old Man led her to a part of the stream that had solid ground all the way to the edge. Breeze knelt down on the bed of yellow aspen leaves and leaned toward the water. Such a soothing sound. On particularly tough days as a child she liked to lie next to a stream just a little way out of town and let it sing her a calming lullaby. *Strange*, she thought, as the stream came into view. *If it weren't for all the rocks, weeds, and turns interrupting the waters path, it wouldn't sing as it does. The water would roll forward unhindered, and silent.*

Reaching down, she buried her hands in the cold water and brought it to her face. The mud began falling from her face and into the stream, which carried it away. Again and again, she brought the cleansing water to her face until she began to feel the smoothness of her own skin and not the grit of the mud. She couldn't believe that one fistful of mud could be so hard to remove. It was in her hairline, her nostrils, and the little folds of her ears. Finally, she was done. She sat back on her heels, released a sigh of relief and opened her eyes.

The Old Man had been sitting next to her, patiently waiting for her to finish.

"Do you want to know yourself?" he asked.

The question caught her completely off guard and sounded, well, a little foolish. Of course, she knew herself. How could a person not know themselves?

The Old Man responded as if she had spoken out loud. "If you knew yourself, you wouldn't feel the way you do." He paused. "And you wouldn't react to Drake the way you do."

He watched Breeze's face as she struggled to comprehend what he had just said.

"Do you want to know yourself?" he asked again.

Breeze wasn't sure she knew the answer to that question, but she was curious to know if what the Old Man had said about her was true.

"Yes," she answered uncertainly.

"Good," he replied, and began marching up the hill. "Follow me."

Breeze hurried to keep up with the Old Man. The pace the Old Man set suggested he knew exactly where he was going, but the various twists and turns he took made her feel hopelessly lost. As her breath began to be short and her legs burned, she began to question herself. What if she didn't really want to know herself? What if what the Old Man said wasn't true of her, and she was really just as ugly on the inside as she felt on the outside? She would have turned back, but she was so turned around she knew she wouldn't have made it. She was also embarrassed to tell the Old Man she didn't want to know herself, whatever that meant, after all.

They appeared in a clearing in the woods, and Breeze jumped. Surrounding them in a circle were twelve women. They stood straight and tall, shoulder to shoulder, eyes closed and bodies still, seemingly lifeless except for the color in their faces.

"Well, this is where I leave you," chimed the Old Man.

"What?" Breeze felt pale.

"I can't come with you on this part of the journey. You have to choose a guide. I will see you on the other side, though." He turned to walk away through a small gap in the circle of women.

"Wait!" Breeze grabbed his wrist. "You can't leave me here. I don't know these women. What if they spring alive and kill me?"

She thought for a moment he was trying not to laugh, but this was not funny. "Breeze," he said calmly, prying her fingers off his wrist. "These women are not going to hurt you. One of them will be your guide."

"Guide to where? Guide to what? I thought we were on some ridiculous journey to know myself." She said the last few words mockingly.

"Yes, well, I'm off," he said and walked out of the circle of women. Breeze started to rush after him, but the circle mysteriously closed even though none of the women had moved.

"How am I supposed to know which one of them will be my guide?" she called after him.

She couldn't see him because the women were so tall but she could hear his answer as he called back to her, "You will know."

"Ugh!" Breeze clenched her fists in frustration. Sometimes she hated that Old Man. After a few deep calming breaths, Breeze started to look around at the circle of women. They were all different in appearance, though all were about a head taller than she was, causing her to look up to see them. Their clothes varied as did their facial features and hair color, but there was something uncannily similar about them all. They radiated a peace and serenity that began to reach inside her, stilling her. The more she studied their faces, the calmer she became.

Not knowing what to do next, she walked up to one of the living statues.

"Um," she tentatively began, "will you be my guide?"

Nothing.

Breeze felt strangely hurt and rejected. She walked on a little way and randomly chose another woman. This time she reached out to touch the woman's hand. It was warm and soft but unmoving.

"Will you be my guide?"

No response.

Hurt began to turn into frustration. She marched up to the next woman, put her face as close as she could reach and petulantly demanded, "How about you? Want to be my guide?" When there was no response again, Breeze impulsively poked the woman in the nose.

Stillness.

She immediately regretted her childish behavior. *Stop it,* she reprimanded herself. She closed her eyes and again took a few deep, steadying breaths. When she opened them again, she began carefully scanning each woman's face. This time she paid attention to how she felt as she looked at each woman. Her eyes came around to a woman with curly red hair that sprang up from her head and cascaded in waves down her back. Her dress was the color of deep summer, embroidered with gold. Breeze didn't particularly like redheads as a general rule, but something inside her shifted as she gazed at this woman. Her feet moved her closer. Not quite knowing why, she lifted her right hand and placed it on her own heart. Her left hand trembled as she placed it over the heart of the red-headed woman.

"I want to know myself." She realized in that moment that what she said was true. "Will you be my guide?" The humility in her own voice surprised her.

The woman's hand covered Breeze's and her eyes opened.

"Yes," she said. "Come."

Chapter Twenty-One

AKING BREEZE'S HAND firmly in hers, the guide left the circle and began walking toward the entrance to a cave just a few feet away.

"Wait," Breeze called out. "Please, will you tell me your name first?"

"Liora," her guide replied. "Come."

Darkness momentarily engulfed Breeze as she entered the cave. She could smell that there was water nearby and feel the coolness of the cave air. As her eyes adjusted she could see a dirt path in front of her that led to a small pool. Inside the water she could see globes of colorful light glowing just beneath the surface.

"Where are we?" Breeze asked, in awe.

Her guide didn't answer but moved along the path toward the pool.

Turning back to Breeze she said, "You will go into this water as you came into the world."

Breeze drew even with her guide. "I came into this world naked," Breeze laughed.

Silence.

Seeing the look on Liora's face, Breeze grew serious.

"I won't do it."

"You don't have to."

Breeze was relieved but also confused. Was it really that easy? *Alright then,* thought Breeze, and took a step toward the water.

Liora's hand on her elbow stopped her.

"You do not have to go into the pool, but if you go in, you will go in as you came into the world."

"I have no idea what's in that water," Breeze said accusingly, "and you want me to just dive in naked."

"Everyone who enters these waters feels fear, but only those with great courage deserve to know the secrets you will find here. Besides," Liora added almost as an after-thought, "you won't be naked. There are cloaks hanging over here on the wall." She gestured to a row of brown cloaks draped on pegs protruding from the cave wall. "When you were born someone must have been there for you to swaddle and care for you. Likewise, you will not go into these waters alone and unprotected."

Breeze stared hard at the water and the luminescent globes just beneath the surface. *Was it worth it?*

She glanced at her guide for some clue to answer her question, but Liora kept her gaze fixed forward, waiting politely for Breeze to make up her mind.

No point living in ignorance, Breeze thought. *If I really am as worthless as Drake makes me feel, I might as well find out now.*

Liora's eyes were fixed firmly ahead so, with a last cautionary look around, Breeze began to undress. When her clothes were folded neatly in a pile at her feet, she walked over and removed a cloak from the wall. She wondered briefly of the others who had worn these cloaks and taken this journey. The softness reminded her of the cloth the old man had given her and the color reminded her of rich, brown dirt. She wrapped the cloak around herself and felt a calmness settle into her heart.

"I'm ready, I suppose."

Liora gestured towards the pool. "Come."

The water was neither cold nor hot. It was not pleasant or unpleasant.

It just was. The farther she walked into the water, the more Breeze felt that there was something familiar about this place.

"What are these globes?" Breeze asked, looking at the glowing spheres in the water.

"These globes represent the hearts of man."

Breeze looked at them more closely. Each one had indistinct colors swirling beneath a cloudy surface.

"How will I know which one is mine?"

"You will know."

As Breeze continued walking, the ground beneath her sloped down causing the water to rise higher and higher around her body. She barely noticed the water rising because she was so distracted by searching desperately for her globe. *Watch,* she thought bitterly, *I'm going to be the first person who comes here who can't find her own heart.*

And then she was underwater. Panic rose as her body descended. The globes grew distant overhead as she sank deeper and deeper. Her arms and legs flailed uselessly but she didn't know how to swim. As her lungs began to burn, fear, anger, and resentment seethed into her soul. In that moment she hated everyone, including herself, and the part they played in bringing her here.

Then something grabbed her elbow, and she felt herself rising to the surface. The moment her face broke the surface of the water she began gasping for breath. Liora released the gentle grip that had pulled her out. After a few minutes of choking and heaving great gasps of air into her lungs she turned on Liora.

"You! You almost let me drown!"

Liora gazed back at her serenely without replying.

What was with this woman? Didn't anything ever make her upset?

"Of course, I get upset," Liora calmly replied as if Breeze had spoken out loud. "However, I choose not to participate in conversations where things are said that are not true and you," she paused and looked pointedly at Breeze, "said something that was not true."

"Well then, what do you call that?" Breeze demanded, gesturing angrily to the deep water she had just been pulled from. "Splashing in a puddle?"

"I call it despair, and you got lost in it. But you're better now—so let's continue."

Breeze didn't want to continue, but she didn't want to quit either. She began looking more intently at each globe. *Surely, she would know her own heart…right?*

And she did. From the moment she saw it. She knew it was her heart because it was the only one she could see clearly. All the other globes had colors that swirled indistinctly behind a sort of mist. The colors of her globe were vibrant, each individual color showing clearly through the glass surface.

Breeze scooped it reverently out of the water and held it in awe. It was beautiful, she realized. She loved it. The colors all ran in a smooth line from the south to the north of her globe. As she stared, mesmerized, she began to understand that the colors were telling a story—her story. She could see within the globe a memory flash by and from that memory would spring an array of different colors. Some memories produced very little color and faded quickly. Other memories, though brief, created a splash of colors that lasted much longer. There was such a beautiful variety of colors—lavender, turquoise, gold, navy, rose—so many different colors Breeze could hardly keep track of them all.

"What do these colors mean?" she asked Liora.

"These colors represent the emotions that are created with each experience."

Breeze noticed one color that she didn't love. It was faint and infrequent, but still there and it bothered her.

"Why are these black lines here? They look so ugly next to the other colors."

"The black lines are the seven common flaws of the human race: pride, resentment, selfishness, dishonesty, envy, self-hatred, and self-pity."

"If there are seven different flaws why are they all the same color?"

"Because they all stem from fear and end in anger and therefore need no differentiation."

"Why do the colors sometimes seem to fade? Sometimes they are so clear and sometimes I can barely see them."

"The colors fade when you are in denial about one of your experiences."

"What do you mean?" Breeze asked.

"Do you have thoughts or feelings that are uncomfortable and so you push them away and avoid dealing with them?"

"I-I don't know," stammered Breeze. "I don't think I have ever paid attention to whether I was doing it or not." Breeze was feeling put on the spot, like she was in trouble. "But sometimes you have to block out thoughts so you can function. Sometimes as an apothecary, it's not good if you think too much about what you are doing, or you wouldn't have the heart to do it."

"This is true," her guide agreed, and Breeze felt a small sense of victory. "But denial is a form of dishonesty. It has a numbing effect. When you block out the things you don't want to think or feel, you block out everything, including the joy."

Disturbed, Breeze turned her attention back to the globe. She loved watching the colors race along. Some colors were bright and airy, others strong and bold, but they were all beautiful. She loved to watch them, except the black.

Without warning, the black color exploded and spread like poison across the inside of the globe. Breeze shouted and nearly dropped the glass ball. The blackness blocked out the other colors, making them weaker and less vibrant. The variety of colors faded until just a few were left, struggling desperately to be seen in spite of the black that covered almost every inch of the glass surface.

"No," Breeze whispered, her heart sinking. Turning to Liora, she pleaded, "Please…please, bring the colors back."

"I can't," Liora replied and Breeze saw there were tears in her eyes.

Breeze pleaded, "Where do I go? What do I do?"

"You will need to take your heart to the Old Man."

"The Old Man?" Breeze asked puzzled.

"Yes," Liora responded, slightly amused now. "Did you think he was just an annoying old man?"

Breeze was too embarrassed to answer that question. "Let's go then," she said. Clutching the globe to her heart, she quickly waded through the water. But something caught her eye—it was another globe. Instead of being misty like all the rest it was crystal clear, like hers.

"What is that?" she asked Liora, confused. "How can I see that heart?"

Liora looked to where Breeze was pointing and a startled look crossed her face. "You have been given a rare gift," she said. "You have been given the ability to see someone else's heart. I suggest you go look."

Cautiously, Breeze approached the globe. The first thing that caught her attention was that it looked so similar to hers. Some of the colors were different but some were exactly the same. She thought for a moment she would like to meet this person, she would probably like them. She smiled as she watched the colors race joyfully along. Then the darkness came in.

"No," she said. Her heart ached for this person. She wanted to save them from the darkness she had witnessed in her own heart, but she could only watch helplessly as the inky blackness spread, obliterating all the joyful colors.

"Can we bring this heart, too?" she pleaded with Liora. "It needs help."

"No, only the owner of this heart can bring it to the Old Man."

"Well, whose is it? How can we know?"

The knowing look in Liora's eyes sent a shiver down Breeze's spine. She looked back at the globe and gazed at it more intently.

Drake.

Both globes began to tremble in Breeze's hands. *No! This wasn't possible. His heart was nothing like hers! HE was the problem! There was no light in him!*

Then as quickly as the anger sprang up, it died. Only sadness remained and she cried. His heart had been beautiful and there was light in him. She knew it and she cried for him.

A gentle hand on her shoulder reminded her she was not alone.

"Come, it is time to go see the Old Man."

After a brief pause to put on her clothes, Breeze left the cave with her guide. Light blinded Breeze as she stepped out of the cave and into the daylight, still clutching her globe to her chest. The Old Man was waiting for her with a smile on his face. She found herself trying to hide her globe. He had said she would come to know herself and she did, but now she didn't want to share it. She wished she could show him the globe before the blackness exploded inside. It was beautiful then, so full of color and light. But now it wasn't, and she was ashamed. She didn't want him to see her pride, anger, fear, and self-pity.

Breeze stood before the Old Man without looking at him. Silence was like a solid wall between them. The Old Man said nothing, only patiently waited. Breeze trembled inside. She wasn't sure why, but she desperately wanted the Old Man to be proud of her. But surely he couldn't, not when he saw all the blackness. Fear seized her heart. Would he stop talking to her? Would he take away her key? True, half the time she was furious with him, but she wasn't ready to never speak to him again.

Liora was there beside her. She put one arm around Breeze and put her other hand under Breeze's globe where she clutched it to her chest. With gentle pressure on Breeze's hand, she guided the globe out into the open space between them and the Old Man. The Old Man placed his hand under both of theirs so that all three together were supporting the globe. Breeze kept her eyes fixed on the ground. The Old Man and Liora continued to wait patiently. The longer she stood there the angrier she became with Drake. Her mind stewed and boiled with the way he had treated her until she blurted out. "It's all Drake's fault! He caused this blackness. I didn't feel like this before I met him! I was happy, and I was kind!"

The Old Man's tender response silenced her. "Blame never helped anyone heal." She looked into his eyes for the first time since leaving the cave.

She saw love. It was clearly written on the Old Man's face. It was unmistakable. It wasn't pride. He wasn't proud of her, but he wasn't ashamed of her either. She searched his face, trying to understand and as she did an assurance flowed over her. *I simply love you.* She had never felt anything like it. It was a love that existed above and outside of her accomplishments, her appearance, her victories, and her failures. This was a love that was immovable. As she looked deep into the Old Man's eyes, she couldn't help but feel the same way about herself.

He finally spoke. "You may not understand this, but I have known you all along. I have seen all your colors from the very beginning. I knew you before you were hurt and the darkness spread. I will know you still when the blackness fades and your colors shine bright again."

"How?" Breeze cried out desperately. "How will I get rid of the blackness?"

"You will never get rid of all of it. To some extent it is the price we pay to live in this world. But you and I will work together to bring your colors back a little at a time and to let go of the darkness so that it gradually fades into the background."

"What do I do? Tell me and I will do it. I promise."

"It will be harder than you think for you to keep that promise, so do not make it lightly. But, for now, you have had a long journey, and you need your rest."

Chapter Twenty-Two

BREEZE SLEPT FROM the time the Old Man released her back into her world until early the next morning. She awoke bursting with energy—and anxiety. What was going to happen with her and Drake? Should she go see him? What would she say? Would he come see her? Her apprehension about the future propelled her out of bed and down the stairs, even though the sun had barely begun to spread a glimmer of light in the sky.

She lit a candle and sat in her father's workroom at the same table where they had saved Drake's leg. All that work, a successful save, and here she still was. Still married in secret and more unsure of her future than ever. She popped up off the chair like a cork off a bottle and began to pace around.

"What a mess," she muttered to herself as she glanced around the room, realizing with a start that this, at least, was a problem she could solve. When her father came downstairs over an hour later, as the sun was just finishing its job of turning night to day, his entire workroom was almost completely unrecognizable. Jars were lined up in precise rows. Knives, cutting boards, mortars and pestles were scrubbed clean. If there was a speck of dust left anywhere in the shop it was hiding for fear of annihilation.

Galen sat down slowly, his jaw hanging uselessly down. Breeze, who felt considerably calmer, beamed at her dad.

"What do you think?"

"My sweet daughter, what have you done?" he asked, his voice choking as he spoke.

"I reorganized and cleaned the shop, of course," she said, confused by her father's reaction.

"I have customers coming today. I have remedies to complete, some of which take days to prepare, and I can't see them anywhere." Tension rose in Galen's body and Breeze could hear a hint of panic in his voice.

"It may take some getting used to but things will be better this way. I promise," she assured him.

"I need you to talk to me," Galen said, shaking his head as if to clear the fog. "You have almost completely disappeared from the shop over the last several months. You have neglected your responsibilities here, sometimes leaving customers mid-interaction. Now I come downstairs to find that you have completely rearranged a shop that has been running, with an abundance of customers I might add, just fine for 20 years. Please, I am begging you, talk to me."

Her initial reaction was to brush her dad off with a cooked-up excuse, but then she remembered her boundary. She had told Drake she would tell her parents and so now she could. Her heart began pounding and her palms felt cold. She knew her father to be kind, but she didn't want to see the hurt in his eyes when he found out. Just imagining it made her heart ache.

Just then, her mom came into the room.

"Breeze, honey, would you like some breakfast? I made eggs and bread."

"No, thank you, mom. My stomach doesn't feel quite right."

They all turned when they heard a knock on the door and saw Caroline come into the back.

"Good day, I am just bringing a treat for Breeze," Caroline said shyly, holding out an apple tart glazed with honey. Breeze was surprised to see her friend as they hadn't spoken much since her first night ride with Drake.

"Thank you, Caroline. This looks amazing. It's exactly what my stomach needs." Breeze brought the apple tart to her mouth.

"I suppose you've all heard the news," Caroline continued.

"No," Galen responded dryly, looking sideways at Breeze. "We've been a little tied up here."

"Please, share," Breeze's mother added warmly.

"Well, there's good news and bad. The bad news is that Father Paul passed away last night. The good news is that Drake and Elaine are finally betrothed. I just saw the notice posted on the church door as I came here this morning."

Breeze suddenly felt as if the apple tart were choking her. She struggled to pull air into her lungs but they wouldn't expand. She could hear a rushing in her ears and her knees went weak.

Everyone noticed at exactly the same time.

"Honey!" her mom cried out. All three rushed to her and helped her to sit down.

Her father's exasperated cry as he searched for the peppermint rang in her ears. A vial was waved in front of Breeze's nose as Galen commanded firmly, "Breathe, Breeze. Breathe it in."

The sharp scent of the peppermint had the desired effect and her lungs obeyed her command to open and inhale. But now she felt trapped. Everyone was too close. Emotions flooded her body and shut down her mind, except for one thought. She needed to find Drake. She could fix this. She needed to make him listen to her. Springing up and pushing past Caroline, Breeze ran through the backdoor, through the garden, and into the woods.

Legs and arms pumping, she pushed herself beyond her limits, hoping desperately that the physical pain would make the emotional pain disappear. Though her lungs and limbs burned, she could still feel and so she kept running. As she ran she prayed desperately that he would be at the shed.

The little wooden structure quickly arrived in her vision, and she burst through the door. Drake sat on the bed, gaze cast down, shoulders hunched. When he looked up, tears streamed down his cheeks.

"Breeze," he cried, "I'm so sorry. I'm so, so, sorry."

"No!" she cried, "Don't be sorry. Do something!"

"I can't! Don't you understand? I've been back in the arena Breeze, and I can't fight like I used to. I'll never win another tournament again."

"You don't know that! Give it time, Drake, please."

"I don't have time. Uncle has been pressuring me to join myself to Elaine for months. I couldn't put him off any longer. Breeze, I'm so sorry."

"No! Stop saying that! Don't give up, please. Don't give up on us. We have options. We can ask my parents for help. We can move to a new town. We're smart and strong and young, Drake. We can make it."

"Stop being so naïve!" Drake said, pounding his fists on their makeshift wedding bed. "It won't work. It's over. I didn't mean for it to end like this, but it did."

"No!" Breeze screamed. "No!"

Drake stood and moved to Breeze. He wrapped her in his arms and pressed her body against the wall with his own, crying into her neck and repeating, "I'm sorry."

"Don't touch me," she sobbed, pounding on his shoulders with her fists but her words were weak and her punches fell harmlessly on Drake's strong shoulders.

Drake kissed her neck one last time and she could feel the wetness of the tears on his cheeks. "I'm sorry," he whispered again, and then he was gone. Breeze collapsed onto their wedding bed, alone. She squeezed the blankets in rage and frustration as she screamed. Something cold and hard was in her hand. The key. She brought it to her chest, her tears changing to ones of gratitude. The Old Man, of course. He could fix this.

"Old Man," she said confidently, "I need you."

Chapter Twenty-Three

HE RIVER WATER *flowed smoothly past the canoe. Warm sunlight pressed itself against the back of Breeze's neck. Tree leaves on the distant riverbanks rustled slightly as if visiting with one another about the beauty of the day. One long wooden oar lay resting across Breeze's knees as the canoe floated serenely down the center of the vast river. Drake sat despairing at the front, head down, one hand clutching the other oar and one hand tangled in his wavy black hair.*

Then she heard it. The rushing of water was rising in volume.

"Drake, we need to start paddling for shore. There is a waterfall up ahead."

"So?"

His response caught her completely off guard. Wasn't it obvious that if a waterfall was up ahead you got off the river?

"We need to start paddling for shore."

"Why? What's the point? We're not going to make it."

Breeze felt a small amount of panic and confusion rising in her chest, but no matter. She still had time to make him understand.

"Of course, we are going to make it, if we start paddling now. Put your oar in the water."

"No."

The distant roar of the waterfall was becoming less distant by the minute.

She could feel, ever so slightly, the urgency of the water increasing as it flowed past the canoe, causing it to pick up speed.

"Drake, put your oar in the water."

He lifted his head now to look directly into her eyes. "Put your own oar in the water."

Breeze realized that she hadn't even thought about putting her own oar in the water because she was so desperately focused on her husband's strange, hopeless behavior. Her face flushed with shame as she jabbed her oar into the water as if it were a solid thing. She began wrestling with the water, but to no avail. It was becoming more and more unruly and the big, unwieldy canoe was built to be operated by two rowers working together. Drake's bulk also pushed the canoe deeper into the water, making it even more difficult to maneuver.

"Drake," Breeze snapped, the panic rising to higher levels now, "you have to help me. I cannot steer this canoe by myself."

"Then don't," was Drake's monotonal reply.

The water was now moving in choppy waves that splashed over the edges of the boat. Breeze continued to wrestle unsuccessfully with her single oar. Her body was beginning to ache from the exertion. The once pleasant sun now felt suffocating. "Why are you going to let us plunge to our deaths without even trying to save us? Put your oar in the water!"

Drake's only response was to lower his eyes back to the floor of the boat.

The panic was full force now. They were so close to the waterfall she could feel the mist in the air. Her mind was racing desperately. How could she get him to start moving? She cast her eyes about wildly, searching for something, anything, that could save them. Then she saw the Old Man. He was standing on the shore gesturing to something behind her.

"Old Man!" she screamed. "Old Man, you have to save us! There is something wrong with Drake! He won't row and I can't do it alone!"

She could tell the Old Man was speaking, but she couldn't hear his response over the now deafening roar of the waterfall. She looked to where he was pointing and saw a small rowboat floating down the river toward them.

Strangely, it floated across the choppy waters right to her canoe. When she reached out and grabbed it she heard the Old Man's voice clearly, as if he were standing right next to her, "Get in the boat."

Confusion overwhelmed her. This boat was tiny, obviously only big enough for one person. There was no way she and Drake would both fit. She heard his voice again, "Get in the boat."

"No!" she screamed. "No!" She shoved the boat away from her, but it bounced back against the side of the canoe. This couldn't be his answer. Breeze looked down and saw that she and Drake were both getting wet now from the splashing waves. The canoe bucked and rolled so wildly she wondered if maybe they would both drown before they even reached the deadly waterfall. But Drake sat unmoving, as if oblivious to it all.

"Drake, please!" Breeze begged, her voice breaking on her sobs. "Please, help me row." No response.

She heard it again. "Get in the boat, Breeze."

Her heart ripped as she leapt from the canoe and into the rowboat. Gripping both handles of the oars affixed to either side, she immediately began maneuvering the tiny boat toward the shore. Her ragged breath tore past the knot in her throat and pushed its way into her chest. Muscles cried out in agony as she battled the river which had lost all sense in its eagerness to plunge over the edge. From one second to the next Breeze didn't know if she would make the safety of the river bank. Finally, the rowboat found a small amount of peace in the slower moving waters near the shore. With a few more exhausted pulls the nose of the boat dug into the river bank. Breeze immediately turned around. The canoe had just reached the edge of the waterfall. Drake lifted his head to look around. As the front of the canoe began to dip over the edge and start its deadly plunge, Drake's eyes found Breeze. "You left me," they said, and then he was gone.

"No!" Breeze didn't think it was possible to feel such pain and still live. It was then she noticed the Old Man standing on the river bank holding onto the little boat to prevent it from slipping back into the tumultuous river.

Rage exploded inside her. Leaping into the water, she charged toward the Old Man.

"You!" she pushed him hard with both hands. "That was your solution?" she demanded. "You are worthless!" she yelled, pushing him again.

The Old Man stood calmly, making no attempt to retaliate or defend himself.

"Drake didn't want to be saved," he said simply.

"What?" Breeze cried hysterically. "Of course, he wanted to be saved!"

The Old Man answered nothing.

"You know what?" Breeze's voice seethed with anger. "I hate you. I hate you, and I wish I would have stayed in the canoe." This sudden realization broke her. She sank onto the muddy shore and cried.

The Old Man sat in the mud next to Breeze and put his arm firmly around her shoulders.

"It was the right thing to do to get in the boat, not just for you. It was the right thing for your child."

Breeze woke with a start. Her body ached as if she really had paddled her way out of imminent death. She wiped the tears from her cheeks.

"My child?" she murmured sleepily. Her heart momentarily stopped and then started bucking furiously like an untamed colt. Her mind raced back searching for when she last experienced her monthly time. How long had it been? Things with Drake had been so chaotic she hadn't time to pay attention to something that seemed so insignificant.

She placed her hand on her abdomen as if questioning it for the answer. My child?

But what now? If she was pregnant, there was not a single soul alive that could vouch for her and Drake's marriage. Drake had the power to completely destroy her life with his selfishness and dishonesty. Breeze had never felt so powerless, or so alone.

Chapter Twenty-Four

WINTER'S TURN WAS nearly over, but it didn't agree. Frozen water troughs still had to be broken so that animals could drink, tired mamas still had to brave chilly floors to stoke a midnight fire and tired papas still had to force iron axes through stone-hard wood.

Breeze's body still showed no signs of its normal rhythm.

One morning, Breeze stood clutching the counter in the front of the shop trying to control the rising bile in her throat. Her mother came in and put a soothing hand on her back.

"Would you like some breakfast, dear?"

Breeze's body shuddered at the thought.

"Please, mama, don't say that word," Breeze said through clenched teeth. "I'll be fine."

After a pause, Darla said, "You haven't eaten well in weeks. You're shrinking so much your bones are sticking out."

Breeze turned her body slightly away from her mom and hunched her shoulders. If her mom had carefully scrutinized Breeze she might have noticed that there was one part of Breeze's body that wasn't shrinking.

"Mama, please, I'll be fine. There are customers," Breeze added as she saw two women walk into the shop.

"I will leave you to it then," her mom responded as she returned to the kitchen.

The women were ornately dressed with jewels dripping from their ears and hanging from their necks. There were poofs and piles of satin and lace all over their bodies. It was not common to see that kind of wealth in Northwell and Breeze recognized them at once. It was Elaine's mother and aunt.

"Good day, young lady," Elaine's mother began. "I am here to make sure I get a grandchild!" she said and both women erupted into laughter.

Breeze immediately heard a rushing sound in her ears and felt a quivering in her chest.

"So, of course, you know what we will need," the mother of the soon-to-be-bride said. "We will need some mandrake root for the tea and some parsley to plant in the garden. If I don't have a grandbaby on the way by the time that parsley blooms I am coming back for my money!"

More laughter. It grated on Breeze's ears. Her constricted throat couldn't make a sound so she wrestled a small smile onto her face and nodded briefly to show she understood the humor.

"We will also need some saffron and fenugreek to leave on the wedding bed." The two women gave each other knowing looks and Breeze broke.

"You'll have to excuse me, I'm sorry." Breeze rushed into the back room. "Dad—customers. I can't," was all she could say before she escaped out the back door and into the frozen garden where a layer of frost covered the barren ground. Tears began to flow freely as she searched for a place to escape. She didn't want to go toward the bakery, or to the shed, so she walked around to the front of the shop. With her head down to hide the tears, she began walking briskly down the town's main street.

Before long, Breeze heard a familiar hammering sound and looked up to see that she was at the smithy. Boulder was holding a piece of bright red metal with tongs and repeatedly striking it, his massive arms wielding the hammer with force and precision. Each time Boulder brought the hammer down, the metal cried out with a painful ring, and sparks exploded like red hot tears. Again and again, he struck the metal and Breeze began to feel each blow in her chest, flinching with each violent swing.

"Stop it!" she screamed. "Please, Boulder, stop it!" Breeze rushed into the shop and grabbed Boulder's arm in a vice-like grip. The hot metal dropped into the dirt, ruined.

Silence. Boulder stood still, his arms glistening with sweat and his chest rising and falling from exertion. The metal faded gradually back to gray and Breeze noticed for the first time that it looked oddly like a flower petal.

"Why are you doing that?" she asked, her arms clutched across her chest and tears streaming down her face.

She could see the confused look on Boulder's face. He knew that she knew the answer. But she didn't want it to be the answer. Hesitating, he gave what they both knew to be the truth.

"Putting metal in the fire and then repeatedly striking it is how we transform the metal from something useless to something useful. Or in this case," he added quietly looking at a table near the forge, "something beautiful."

A half-finished metal rose sat on the table.

"But why?" Breeze cried, "why can't you be gentle?"

Boulder knew for certain now that whatever Breeze was talking about had nothing to do with the properties of metal.

"I don't know," he said simply, staring into Breeze's eyes. She could see the kindness in them as he added, "It requires heat and force to transform the metal. It's just the way things are."

Walking over to the metal rose, Breeze sank down onto a wooden bench and stared at it. Boulder came and sat quietly beside her. They sat together without touching or talking for some time.

Drake's voice broke the silence. "Boulder, I am looking for Breeze, and I was told she was here."

Breeze and Boulder simultaneously turned towards the sound of Drake's voice. As Drake's eyes adjusted to the dim light he saw Breeze and Boulder sitting side by side. His eyes went dark and the muscles in his jawline drew taut.

"I see." Spinning sharply on his heel, Drake disappeared. Breeze shot out of the smithy after him.

"Drake!" she called towards his receding back. "Please, Drake! Talk to me!"

Drake abruptly stopped and whirled around to face Breeze. "I had something to tell you, something important, but it doesn't matter now." His eyes, burning with anger, glanced back toward the smithy where Boulder was standing in the door way. "I should have known." And with that he was gone, striding down the street, back stiff and head high.

Breeze wrapped her arms tightly around herself and looked around. Her eyes landed on Boulder whose huge frame filled the door of the smithy. She could tell by his expression he had heard their interaction. Too embarrassed to go back in, she began to slowly make her way home.

Breeze walked with her head hung down, her shoulders bent over and her arms clung to her waist as if trying to hold herself together. A thought, a spark, lit up in her mind.

How dare he?

What started as nothing more than an ember grew as Breeze found fuel in her mind to throw on the fire.

How dare he accuse me? How dare he abandon me, betray me, and then accuse me of being like him?! Coward! I am nothing like him!

The fire roared in her chest and the more she fed it, the more it flamed and burned.

He convinces me to marry him in secret and then refuses to stand up to his uncle and make our marriage known, refuses to even try *to save it! Filthy, rotten, useless, selfish coward! And he has the audacity to accuse me?!*

The fire reached up into her mind and began to consume her reason.

I am going to blast his name from here till the end of creation. I will make sure he never *competes in another tournament again. I am going to take this child after it is born and place it in Elaine's ugly, white arms and tell her every detail of how this child was conceived right under her perfect nose.*

By the time Breeze reached home her common sense had burned completely away and disappeared like smoke into the sky. Charging into her little shop she began grabbing vials, jars and bottles and smashing them one right after the other on the wooden floor. Sharp, awful scents of remedies that should never have been mixed together reached into her nose but still didn't extinguish the fire and restore her reason.

Her mother and father came rushing into the shop. Even her father's horrified cry as he saw months and months of hard work shattered on the floor couldn't rise above the roaring fire in her ears. Galen and Darla sprang forward and grabbed their daughter, finally bringing her back to her senses.

Breeze looked around as if coming out of a nightmare. She saw one vial still clenched in her upraised hand and her father's white knuckled grip on her throbbing wrist. She saw the carnage of herbs, oils and glass on the floor.

"Oh, Dad," she whispered. "Dad, I'm so sorry."

Her father couldn't answer. He could barely move for fear of what he would do to his daughter if he did. With great effort he released her wrist and through clenched teeth commanded, "Go upstairs." Breeze fled the room.

As soon as she reached the top of the stairs she sank to the floor. She wanted so desperately to call for the Old Man. She wanted to feel his gentleness and his strength, but she was ashamed. She didn't want him to know what she had done. Even more she didn't want him to know how she felt—her burning hatred for Drake. So, she sat on the floor and hugged her knees to her chest, feeling more alone than she ever had before. Then she remembered his words: *"I have known you all along."* He would understand. He would still love her, and she needed him. She quickly crawled across the floor, grabbed the key from off her desk, pressed it to her forehead and whispered, "Old Man, I need you."

Chapter Twenty-Five

SHE WAS STANDING somewhere, but she didn't know where. She didn't care. Nothing mattered except the globe she cradled in her trembling hands. It was cracked. Not just one crack, hundreds of them splintering across the surface. The blackness inside was dripping out, staining her hands, sliding between her fingers and falling to the ground, lost. Only one color remained, a deep rose red that she glimpsed briefly as it intermittently fought its way to the surface.

But it was also leaking out, and she knew that unless something changed, her globe would be empty. There would be no anger, no hurt, no fear. There would also be no joy, no pleasure, no peace. There would be nothing. Just a shattered, empty representation of what her heart used to be.

"Please," she whispered to the globe. "Please, hold on." She tried to will the globe to seal its cracks. Nothing. She couldn't remember another time in her life when she had felt so powerless. She was raised by a gifted apothecary. There was always a solution, an herb, an ointment. You just had to figure it out and when you did, people were healed.

"Heal," she begged the globe. "Please, heal."

"It doesn't work that way." The Old Man appeared by her side. "The globe can heal," he continued, "but it's something we do together."

"I don't understand. Why can't I just do it myself?"

"Some of it you can. Some of it we do together and sometimes it just comes as a gift from me, to you. For example, may I hold your globe?" he asked, reaching out his hands.

Not knowing why, Breeze felt apprehensive.

"What are you going to do to it?"

"I'm going to heal the cracks so it stops leaking."

Like a living thing, fear leapt into her chest, grabbing her throat and kicking her stomach. Healing the cracks suddenly seemed like a terrible idea, the worst she had ever heard. It made sense to her now why it was all leaking out. The process was ugly, but when it was finished, she would be safe. Safe from any more blackness. After all wasn't it the colors that let the darkness in? Wasn't it love and passion that ruined everything?

Was it love? Could she have possibly loved Drake? She thought back on the love she had felt from the Old Man after she shared her heart. He had seen all of her heart, and he loved her, not in spite of it, but because of it. She had barely known Drake when she married him. She had fallen in what she thought was love with a dream of him she had conjured up in her mind. Had she really taken the time to see his heart completely? Did he take the time to see hers? Or had they both been using each other? Had she used Drake to satisfy her pride, to feel important? Had he used her to silently rebel against his uncle and assert his freedom?

It didn't matter now. Blackness continued to seep out of her globe and onto her hands. In just a few moments she would feel nothing. She would want nothing and need no one. She would be safe. The leaking globe now seemed just as it should be. It was leaking to protect her.

Her trembling, blackened hands became very still and her breathing slowed.

"No," she said. "No, I don't think that's a good idea." The fear inside her loosened its grip. It was simple really. All she had to do was go numb, and she would never hurt again.

This was only the second time she had ever seen true pain in the Old Man's eyes.

"Drake left you, you know." The Old Man's voice was calm, like always, but it was firmer than she had ever heard it.

Her eyes flashed. "I know that!" she snapped.

"He quit on you. Shame on him," he continued in the same firm tone. "But if you quit on yourself, then shame on you."

Just like in the cave, she heard love. She heard it and she felt it. She knew she was being reprimanded, but she didn't feel defensive. She just felt love.

"Do you see that little bit of red left in your globe?" the Old Man asked.

Breeze gave a small nod.

"That red is courage," he told her. "There is still a little left. Will you use it?"

Breeze couldn't speak. She could feel fear starting in with its violent warnings, grabbing her throat, choking her air, but fear was not her master.

She gave a small nod.

"How did it make you feel when Drake refused to try to save your marriage before he left you?" he asked.

"You know that," she whispered.

"Say it out loud," he prodded.

"Worthless." The word dropped into the air like a shameful, ugly thing.

"Will you let me give you something?"

Another nod.

The Old Man moved to place his hands under Breeze's but she jerked back.

"You can't," she said, "your hands will get dirty, like mine."

"I accept that," he responded.

She held her hands out again, and the Old Man placed his hands under hers, the blackness staining them both.

The moment the Old Man touched her a vision came into her mind and she closed her eyes, looking inward. She saw herself, dressed in a simple white robe and standing calmly, a small smile on her face, but it was what she suddenly knew that amazed her. She knew as she gazed at herself that she was of great worth. This knowledge was so unlike anything she dreamed of as a little girl, when she would dream that her hair was thicker, her skin smoother, or her lips redder so that she could attract more attention. It wasn't like her dreams as she grew, that she would become so skilled as an apothecary that she would surpass even her father in skill and people would come from distant villages to seek her out. Or, most recently, that she would be of worth because she would have the gorgeous and talented Drake McArthur as her husband.

As she looked at herself in the vision, the woman she saw was so serene. She was not above or below such things—just not a part of them. Her worth seemed constant, like the sun. It just was. Her moods, her feelings, and her circumstances could change like the weather. But her worth was always there.

She opened her eyes and saw that her globe was healed. The blackness was all still there but the cracks were gone. And there was a new color, a beautiful golden yellow that shimmered just below the glass surface.

"How did you do that?" she asked.

"It's called acceptance. The globe is again able to hold all your experiences, both good and bad."

Breeze frowned. "But then how will the darkness come out?"

"It won't come out. Over time the other colors will absorb it. When black is mixed with colors it gives them a beautiful hue. You will see. You might be surprised to find that eventually you will not regret the darkness you have experienced."

Breeze traced her finger along the surface of the globe. The shimmering yellow was beautiful, and she loved the way it contrasted with the rose red as they swirled together.

"How do I get more colors back?

"Well, that depends on what you are willing to give up."

"What do you mean?" she asked.

"Each aspect of the darkness has its opposite. If you want to bring more color into your globe, you have to figure out which aspect of the darkness you are willing to replace."

"I still don't understand."

"If you are feeling fear, you can replace it with trust. If you feel self-pity you can replace it with empowerment; selfishness with compassion; resentment with acceptance; envy with gratitude and generosity; dishonesty with authenticity, and so on."

Breeze, unwilling to look up, rubbed her thumb along one line of blackness. She knew this one.

"What about hatred?" she asked quietly.

"The only cure for hatred is forgiveness." There was no condemnation in his voice. She could tell that he understood what that would take.

Fear began again with its incessant kicking and shouting.

"I can't," she protested. "I have to remember. If I don't remember, he will hurt me again."

"If you don't forgive him, he will hurt you every day for the rest of your life. He will stain every moment and be a partner in every relationship. Is that what you want?"

"I don't think I have a choice. I can't forgive him. I know I can't." Her voice was small, defeated. She wasn't trying to be rebellious or difficult. She just knew her own heart, and forgiveness for Drake wasn't possible.

"You are not a prisoner or a victim. It's your heart. You get to decide what happens with it."

Breeze looked up and into the Old Man's eyes then, testing his words against her feelings, trying to see if she could believe him.

"I know you are still learning if you can trust me, but just as I gave you a knowledge of your worth, I can give you what you would need to forgive. It is not usually a fast process, and it can be quite painful, but the color of forgiveness is stunning and you will not regret adding it to your globe."

"How does it happen?" Breeze asked tentatively, still not sure forgiveness would give more than it would take.

"It is different for everyone and depends on the hurt suffered, but in your case, I believe some compassion would help."

"Compassion?" Breeze asked, sharply drawing back her head.

"I can give you some, if you will let me," the Old Man offered, holding out his hands.

Reluctantly, Breeze held out her heart.

Chapter Twenty-Six

FROM THE MOMENT she realized where she was, she began to panic. It was the shed the day Drake ended their relationship.

But instead of seeing Drake, she realized that she *was* Drake. She was staring down into her own face and could hear his thoughts and feel his feelings. She knew, beyond a shadow of a doubt, that she would never trust the Old Man again.

She felt her own fists landing on his shoulders and heard her sobs in his ears. Then Drake left, and in his mind, she went with him. Her first terrified thought was that he was going to go straight to Elaine's.

"Old Man," she screamed. "Old Man, get me out of here or you will be the one I never forgive!" But her fear subsided when she saw that he was veering toward the stables.

"Balius, old boy, you want to stretch that leg?" Drake greeted the war horse, who gave a friendly nicker in response. Drake ran his fingers along the scar on Balius' shoulder and Breeze felt a deep sense of regret and self-loathing well inside of Drake.

"I'm so sorry, Balius," Drake apologized, softly rubbing the horse's silky black nose. "I've hurt you. I've hurt you, Breeze…I hate myself." His voice broke and Breeze could feel his throat tightening painfully. Drake gave himself a shake and wiped away the tears rolling down his cheeks.

"Stop it, Drake," he told himself. "Nobody cares if you're sorry." Opening the stall door, he clicked for Balius to follow him. Without saddle or bridle, Balius obediently followed Drake out of the stall. As soon as Drake could smell the fresh outside air he vaulted onto the warhorse's wide back. Reaching down he rubbed Balius' injured shoulder. "Nice and slow, right Old Boy? Just to work out the kinks." Balius obediently set out at a slow walk.

Breeze noticed that instead of taking Balius out the main gate and down the road that would lead by her house, he steered Balius toward a back entrance that wound its hidden way toward the outskirts of town.

Drake's thoughts were silent as he set his back towards town, but after travelling for a short while, Breeze felt a swell of emotion as they neared Cob's Hill. Dismounting, Drake sat in the same spot he sat the night he asked Breeze to marry him, but to Breeze's surprise his thoughts did not go to that moment. It wandered far away into the past. In Drake's mind, she saw a woman who had to have been Drake's mother due to their striking resemblance. Her wavy black hair was limp and plastered to the side of her pale face. Her hand in Drake's was disturbingly cold and clammy.

"My son," she was saying, "you have been dealt a hard blow by life, but your children do not need to suffer the same fate. Your father and I, we married for love, and it was a foolish mistake. Your father was a worthy knight, full of skill and valor, but he died," her voice cracked and her breathing became ragged. "He died and left us." She paused and closed her eyes, tears streaming silently down her face.

When she opened her eyes again she locked them onto her youngest son. "Promise me," she pleaded, "promise me you will marry well so that your children will always be provided for. Marry someone who will bring wealth and honor to the great name of McArthur again."

"I promise, Mama."

Relaxing now, she again closed her eyes and laid down her head. "Of all my sons," she continued quietly, "you are the one who can do this. You will be handsome, mark my words. Your mind is sharp and your skill with the sword already surpasses some of your brothers. Use those gifts well, Drake. Do not disappoint me."

"Yes, Mama. I promise."

The memory faded and Drake's mind drifted back to the present.

"Breeze doesn't understand, Balius," Drake said out loud to his warhorse who was munching contentedly on a nearby patch of grass. "She thinks we could be happy, but we can't. Being a knight, keeping my promise, has been my every waking thought since I was eight years old. I could never be happy without it. I would be miserable hobbling around an apothecary shop, smiling at customers and washing her mortar and pestle while she bustles about saving the world. She thinks she wants that, but she doesn't. My misery will ruin her happiness."

Standing, Drake began picking up rocks and hurling them off the hill.

"The difference between Breeze and Elaine is that Elaine won't care if I'm miserable," Drake continued with a rueful laugh. "I can disappear to my corner of the manor house and she to hers. As long as I dress nice, smile nice, and let her show me off at parties she will be satisfied," he finished bitterly.

For a long while, Drake stood motionless, staring out over the valley.

"I was selfish to take Breeze when I did," he said out loud to no one. "She was just so beautiful, and I love the way I feel when I'm around her. If I hadn't gotten hurt, it would have worked like a dream come true and given me more than I deserved. But I know I can't be happy now, and I won't be selfish again. She deserves better than me."

Drake began striding purposefully toward town. "Come on, Balius. Let's go home."

Chapter Twenty-Seven

THE CONNECTION WITH Drake faded gradually until she was once again in her own mind, the Old Man watching closely and patiently.

"Well?" questioned the Old Man. "Did that help?"

"I'm not sure," Breeze responded reluctantly. Her mind felt odd, like a team of horses who won't all pull in the same direction and therefore loses its strength. "I can understand his reasons, but…" she paused, wrestling with the thoughts in her mind to line up and move forward, "but I can't respect them."

To her surprise, the Old Man smiled.

"The good news," he informed her, "is that forgiving and condoning have nothing to do with each other."

The Old Man let Breeze think about that for a moment before continuing.

"Sometimes the minds of those who have harmed us are extremely dark and twisted places and going inside will only cause further harm. But in this situation, I knew that Drake's motivations were partially motivated by emotional wounds and a misguided sense of self-sacrifice."

Breeze gave a small snort. "Misguided is exactly the word for it."

"But, come now," the Old Man countered. "Do you feel even a little less angry than you did before?"

Breeze paused to look inward before responding. "Yes, a little," she admitted.

"And doesn't that feel nice?" asked the Old Man, smiling.

"Yes," she laughed, "a little."

"Now, look." He directed her gaze to her globe.

Beneath the glass surface she saw a new color beginning to appear, the brilliant green of a new leaf. The kind of color you only see in spring when new life is bursting forth upon the Earth. It was just a wisp of color, the tiniest tendril, but it gave Breeze hope to see it.

She looked at the colors in her globe beginning to harmonize like a beautiful melody, yet still so faint she was afraid they would disappear.

"How do I get more colors?" she asked.

"I have found humility to be a lovely addition to any globe," the Old Man replied. "Along with the rich hue of accountability."

Breeze's eyebrows shot up. "Accountability? To who? I was the one who was betrayed."

"Yes," said the Old Man tenderly. "The damage you have suffered is real, but so is the damage you have caused."

"Caused? What are you talking about?" Breeze demanded.

"Will you allow me to show you?" The Old Man held out his hands.

Breeze pulled back and refused to offer her hands. "I'm not going back inside Drake's mind," she said warily.

The Old Man chuckled and continued to hold out his hands.

"This one has nothing to do with Drake."

Breeze said nothing but continued to look skeptically at the Old Man's hands.

"You have my word," he promised.

Breeze held out her hands.

The first scene she saw pierced her heart. Caroline sat staring out the window of the bakery. Breeze knew why she was there. That was the window Caroline looked out of when she was waiting for her friend to come join her, and this was the time of day that she would have been coming. After a few moments, Caroline wiped away a single tear, grabbed her shawl and headed outside and down the street, alone.

The scenes came quickly after the first one. There was scene after scene of her rushing off and abandoning her work at the apothecary, leaving her father to shoulder the burden alone. She saw him late at night, fighting to stay awake as he prepared treatments for his customers, their customers. She noticed for the first time his graying hair, the spots on the back of his hands, and the creases in his face.

She saw her mother, sitting alone at the kitchen table, hands clasped together and pressed to her forehead, tears on her face, and Breeze knew she was praying for her.

She saw Boulder as time and time again she rudely ignored him in her preoccupation with Drake.

The last face surprised her. It was Elaine, smiling adoringly up at Drake the day Breeze saw them in the bakery. For the first time Breeze felt compassion, and even regret, for how her actions could impact Elaine. It was true that Drake and Elaine's betrothal was not yet official but everyone knew there was a level of understanding between them and Breeze felt a profound sense of guilt for participating in deceiving her.

Right when she thought she couldn't feel any worse about herself the Old Man let go of her hands and the vision ended.

Breeze's voice was quiet. "I don't think I have any respect left for myself after what I just experienced." She felt unwilling to lift her eyes to look at the Old Man.

"It's a good thing then that your worth isn't tied to anything you just saw," he said lightly.

Breeze looked up now, searching the Old Man's face, trying to understand what he had just said.

"Those are things you have done," he explained. "They are not who you are."

"I don't understand," she responded. "If I am not a collection of the things I have done, then what am I?"

"You are who you can become. It is for that reason that your worth is constant."

Breeze's mind wandered back to the plant that she wanted to throw away but her dad wouldn't let her. Her dad saw what the plant could become, and for that reason he chose to save it.

"No action exists all by itself," the Old Man continued. "There are the experiences that led to that action, how you felt about that action, and what you plan to do about the action, if anything, once it happens. All these things matter."

"What I plan to do…" Breeze repeated pensively. "What can I do? The damage is already done."

"It is true that there are times when nothing can be done about what is in the past, but we can always make amends by making better choices in the future."

"What if…" Breeze was afraid to say the words out loud because they filled her with an awful sense of loneliness. "What if they won't forgive me?"

"That is a possibility," the Old Man admitted, "but making amends is only partly about the other person. When we make choices that we can believe in, then we are also making amends to ourselves."

Breeze felt a sense of peace settle into her at the thought. She had made a lot of choices that she didn't believe in to protect her relationship with Drake. She felt hope at the thought of being connected to those around her and also to herself again.

"Old Man, it's time for me to go home."

He smiled. "Indeed, it is."

Chapter Twenty-Eight

SUNLIGHT WOKE BREEZE with the lightest caress. Taking stock of herself, she noticed she felt rested, calm, and ready to face the day, which surprised her. She couldn't remember the last time she woke up that way.

Then she remembered that today was the day she was going to make amends. Maybe not, she thought, pulling the covers back over her head. Maybe she would stay in bed and pretend to be sick. *Never mind*, she huffed as she threw off her blankets. Her dad was an apothecary. That would never work.

She stared at the wooden beams in the roof. There was nothing to do but to go downstairs, and for the first time since Drake had walked back into her life, tell her parents the truth.

But how much of the truth? They definitely didn't need to know about the shed, Breeze thought shaking her head. But the baby? Her heart seized in her chest. Her decision to marry Drake and his decision to abandon her was about to profoundly impact her parents lives even though neither of them had participated in either decision.

Maybe she would miscarry, she thought as she walked down the stairs. Then, as if someone had pushed her in a glacial lake, her whole body went cold.

Every herb she would need to end the life inside her was downstairs.

By tonight, at least one aspect of her problem could be gone. She placed a trembling hand behind her and lowered herself onto the stairs, taking deep steadying breaths. She hadn't learned it from her father, not directly. But she had heard him warn pregnant women away from herbs like yarrow and pennyroyal because of their potential to harm and even expel a baby.

She tried to stand but her legs were too weak. She gripped the edge of the stair with both hands, continuing to breathe in and out, in and out.

She couldn't. She just knew she couldn't. No matter what it cost her, she would see this child into life. Pushing off the stair with both hands, she rose and continued her descent. When she reached the bottom of the stairs, she gasped. Galen was slumped over on his work table. Dried herbs in various stages of processing were strewn across the table along with the various tools of the trade.

Breeze rushed over to Galen and then sank to the floor in relief when she felt through her hand on his back his breath coming steadily in and out of his body.

Just then, Darla entered from the kitchen.

"Fell asleep on his work again, did he?" she asked.

Breeze felt a surge of shame at the lack of surprise in her mom's voice. *I can't do this to him,* she thought. *I can't add more harm than I already have. I will just have to wait for a better time.*

At the sounds of his wife's voice, Galen lifted his head and looked groggily around. When his eyes landed on his daughter, he froze for a moment, contemplated his only child, and then silently looked away. It stung Breeze.

"Dear," he addressed his wife, "I would like some breakfast before I get back to work."

"Yes, my love, it's ready," Darla replied warmly.

Such a simple exchange, but it made Breeze's heart ache with loneliness. She had believed with her whole heart that she was going to have with

Drake what her parents had with each other, but now he was gone and she was alone. She wanted to weep and scream with frustration, but then she remembered, this moment wasn't about her. It was about making amends.

Breeze stood up, squared her shoulders, and gave her arms a few good shakes. She felt like she was preparing to slay a dragon and, in a way, she was. It was the dragon of deceit. She had nourished it from the first moment it hatched right inside her own home until it grew to be the beast it was now. That stopped today.

"Dad," she called out to his receding back. "I have something I need to tell you."

He paused but didn't turn.

She opened her mouth to speak and found that she couldn't. How could she say these words to his back? She was trying, but her mouth wouldn't let her form any words.

Her dad turned around to face her, his expression curious. She looked over and saw the love and concern in her mother's eyes. It gave her the courage she needed.

"I have been secretly wed to Drake McArthur since last spring. He is refusing to announce the marriage and is choosing to marry Elaine...and I'm with child."

Nothing. No words. No reaction.

She could see her father's analytical mind hard at work trying to understand what she said. This she expected, but it was her mother's look that hurt the most. Darla was staring at her daughter like she would stare at a stranger.

Just one word from her father, "How?"

"I would rather not discuss the details at this moment. The important thing that I need to say is, I'm sorry. I'm sorry for deceiving you. I'm sorry for abandoning my responsibilities at the shop, and I am especially sorry for the damage I did yesterday. I will work as hard as I can to repair the damage to both your hearts and our family business."

And then she stood, still and quiet. Saying the truth out loud made her face it herself. It was such a sad story she could hardly believe it was hers. She wanted to crumple to the floor and cry out everything she was feeling but she refused. Not out of pride, but because she didn't want to play on her parent's pity. This moment was for them.

In two short strides, Darla had wrapped her daughter in her arms. Before the first tear fell, Galen had joined them. Darla clung fiercely to her only child, as if trying to take all Breeze's pain into herself.

"Thank you for your honesty," Darla whispered.

"We will be here for you, Breeze," her father added.

The connection Breeze felt to her parents in this moment was like a tangible thing in her soul. She felt sure that if she could see her globe right now this connection would be vibrant and pulsating across the entire surface, drowning the black into insignificance. It was the sweetest thing she had felt in a long, long time.

Chapter Twenty-Nine

WINTER FINALLY EXHAUSTED its iron grip and spring burst forth, surging up through the softened ground with new life. After such a long exile, Spring grabbed her pallet and exuberantly painted the earth in a glorious array of color.

Breeze was back in her happy place, dirt on her dress and Mother Nature's healing gifts between her fingers. The rich smell of earth and freshly blooming herbs filled her nose while the playful chatter of birds and the hardworking drone of bees filled her ears. She paused in her work to soak it all in and place a hand over her belly.

The life within her continued to thrive and began to draw the inevitable attention she knew it would. Fortunately for her and her parents, her father was the best apothecary not just in their town but for many towns within many miles. So even though townsfolk may have enjoyed their gossip and felt entitled to their judgements, their sicknesses drew them back to the healing they could find nowhere else.

Even with the great loss she felt at the life she thought she would have, a new and exciting opportunity had come her way which lifted her hopes for the future. Almost as soon as Darla finished hugging her the day she slayed the dragon of deceit, her mother rushed off to fetch the town midwife. The midwife had come regularly after that, more than was necessary in fact, until one day she invited Breeze to be her new apprentice. The midwife agreed she wouldn't have to give up her work at the apothecary, so after consulting with her parents, who both agreed whole heartedly, she set out on a new adventure full of learning and challenges.

With the changes in her body, and the way townsfolk loved to gossip, it was no surprise when Galen came into the garden and in a perfect monotone and masked expression announced, "Drake is here." Breeze looked carefully at her father's face and made a mental note to ask him later about how seeing Drake made him feel.

Drake was pacing rapidly around the shop, picking up random jars and then placing them back on the shelves in haphazard places.

"Breeze, I must speak with you," he announced as soon as he saw her.

"Go ahead," she said lightly, quietly moving about the shop and replacing all the misplaced jars.

"Not here," he snapped, his eyes darting about wildly like a trapped animal.

"I'm not leaving right now. I am at work."

Drakes eyes stopped their frantic movement and landed sharply on Breeze. She wondered briefly if she had ever said no to Drake before. He took a step closer so he was looming over her. His muscular bulk, which before had seemed so attractive, now felt intimidating and even a little frightening.

"Come to me after work then, at the shed. We can speak there." Without waiting for a response, he turned quickly and took a step toward the door.

"No."

He paused.

Breeze was surprised to find that instead of anger, she felt only compassion. She could only imagine what it must be like for him to find out through gossip that he was possibly a first-time father, but she wasn't going to use compassion to make a foolish decision. She could be both compassionate and firm.

"I will not meet you at the shed, for any reason, and after work I am busy."

"Are you going on your silly walks with Caroline?"

Breeze tried to remember if he had always been this condescending or if this was a new behavior now that he was no longer trying to win her.

"No," she responded quietly, dropping her eyes to the floor. "She is not ready to fully renew our friendship, but I go by every evening and we speak for a few minutes, and that is enough for me."

She took a deep breath and lifted her eyes back to meet Drake's. Seeing that he was about to respond she cut him off, "However, this is my home and I will not tolerate you being rude to me here. If you will not speak to me with respect than this conversation is over."

Drake looked at her the same way her mother looked at her on her dragon-slaying day, like she was a total stranger—but this time she relished it and had to force herself not to smile. Then he was hugging her and crying, and she was bewildered, her arms out to the side and her head pulled back, trying to figure out what just happened. But as he held her, she could feel, almost as if it seeped into her body, his genuine sorrow. She ached for his pain. Wrapping her arms around him, she held his body as it shook.

Finally, he pulled back and looked at her, his hands still on her growing waist. "Breeze, I'm so sorry. Will you forgive me?"

Breeze remembered her sweet experience with the Old Man and the beautiful color of forgiveness.

"I forgive you," she said, and she meant it.

He slid his hand around onto her belly.

"We will do what you said. We will try to make it work," he said excitedly.

Breeze felt like every string that connected her to reality had been snipped.

"Drake," she said, firmly removing his hand from her belly. "I said I forgive you. I didn't say I trust you. I'm not sure that I want to have a life with you."

She almost couldn't believe her own ears. Inside she was screaming at herself to take it back and that she didn't mean it, but another part of herself, a deeper part, knew that it was true.

"You didn't think you could be happy with me," she explained. "How is a child going to change that? The only easy thing about children is making them. And besides, what about Elaine?"

"I don't care about, Elaine. I care about you. I always have. I want to grow old with you, Breeze."

Breeze pulled her brows together. She knew she should be flattered but something about what he said wasn't sitting right with her.

"That's an interesting thing to say about a woman you are about to marry," she responded slowly, the wheels in her mind still turning.

"Why should you care about Elaine?" Drake asked. "I'm telling you that you were right and that I'm willing to try. What more could you ask of me?"

"You would do that for me?" Breeze felt a warmth inside at his willingness to sacrifice for her, and why should she care about Elaine? Breeze had a child to think of. But still she hesitated.

"Elaine didn't know about any of this. It's not her fault, and I don't want her to get hurt."

"Breeze, we have a child to think of," Drake countered, echoing her own thoughts. "Besides, I thought you would be happy I was willing to leave her. Weren't you always jealous of her anyway?"

Breeze was silent for a while. She should be happy. Why wasn't she? He was offering her what she had most desperately hoped for. Then she thought of all her conversations with the Old Man, and she knew.

"I don't need her to hurt for me to heal."

And then another thought formed in her mind like a solid foundation for all her hopes to safely rest upon. Her future happiness was not tied to the blazing comet that was Sir Drake McArthur. It was hers, like her plant, to nourish and to grow one tender day at a time.

"And," she continued slowly as she contemplated this new awareness and how good it felt, "I don't need you to fall for me to rise."

Now it was Drake's turn to be silent.

"You are a good woman, Breeze," he finally responded.

"I know."

"Breeze, let me back into your life," he pleaded. "I will honor you, and the child, I promise."

She could see the sincerity in his eyes. She knew he fully intended to keep his promise, but intention and action were two different things. He intended to keep his promise, but would he?

"I can't decide this right now. It's a lot to think about. Give me a couple of days and I will let you know."

"I am getting married in a couple of days," he responded desperately.

"I know," Breeze said, staying calm. "But I won't make this decision rashly. I need some time to think about it."

Drake could tell that no amount of pushing was going to change her mind, so he picked up her hand and kissed it tenderly.

"I love you," he said. "I will be waiting for your response."

Chapter Thirty

BREEZE PULLED HER shawl tighter around her shoulders as she stepped out of the shop into the crisp morning air. She needed to get an early start if she was to meet the Old Man at the top of the mountain today. After her meeting with Drake and when her work was done for the day, she had gone to her room and held the key, telling the Old Man she needed him. Instead of coming to him at once, she felt in her mind that if she would go to the top of the mountain the next day she would see him there. She didn't hear his voice or see him. She just knew that if she went, he would be there.

The cool air woke her lungs as the steady rhythm of her feet set her path towards the mountains. The conversation with Drake from the day before filled her thoughts. She never could have guessed that he would have such a sudden change of heart and it left her feeling confused. She knew she had an important decision to make and the weight of it pressed on her thoughts and crowded her mind. Deep in thought, she almost ran straight into Boulder.

"Good heavens!" she exclaimed placing her hand over her pounding heart.

"Sorry, Breeze." His voice was deep and gentle, like always. She remembered how she had told her Dad that Boulder was like Earth, boring and without passion. Awareness of her present circumstances made her feel she could use a little less passion and a little more Earth in her life.

She laid a hand on his arm. "No, don't apologize. You did nothing wrong." A thought dawned on her and she looked up at him. "Why are you up so early?"

And then he blushed. Which made Breeze feel confused, which made her start blushing. Why was he blushing? And for the love of all that was good and holy, why was *she*?

Boulder opened his mouth to speak but couldn't quite start his sentence. So, they just stood there in the middle of the quiet street in the cool morning air, blushing and staring and silent. Breeze became aware that her hand was still on his arm. She jerked it back as if Boulder himself were one of the hot metals he worked with and in that moment, he found his voice.

"I heard about your situation." He glanced involuntarily at her stomach which made his blush go an even deeper red. Then as if by an unseen force Boulder decided he was done being awkward. He closed his eyes, took a few deep breaths in through his nose and let it flow slowly out through his lips. Breeze watched, almost fascinated, as his enormous chest expanded with each breath and then fell slowly back into place as it was released. When he opened his eyes there was a confidence in their remarkable brown depths that Breeze hadn't seen since Drake had stepped so suddenly into her life.

Reaching out, Boulder took her hand and folded it between his two hands where it almost completely disappeared. He looked steadily into her eyes. His gaze was so open, so connected, that Breeze could feel herself wanting to cry, like a stone wall that cracks from the force of a soft caress.

"I want to be there for you. I want to help you, in any way I can, in any way you will let me. I...I care about you, Breeze."

She wanted to throw herself into his arms. She wanted to be swept away and surrounded by his kindness and protection and born up by his strength.

"Boulder, you honor me. Thank you. But I don't want to be rescued. I want to come to love with something to offer, something to give, and right now, I am broken and my healing has just barely begun…"

"I can help heal you, Breeze, I can be there for you. I want to marry you." His voice was urgent, almost pleading.

Breeze reached up and laid her hand on the side of Boulder's face, feeling his soft black stubble beneath her fingers. "If I had more sense, Boulder, I would have seen you there all along. But I didn't and now," she glanced down the road that led out of town and to the mountain, "now I have a journey to take before I can be whole again. Good day, Boulder."

With that Breeze tucked her shawl back around her waist and started down the dirt road to the mountain.

Within a short distance, the grassy meadows outside of town began to give way to a rocky trail that led up the mountain. A cold stream followed the path and kept her company with its splashing and babbling as she climbed. Breeze settled into a steady pace, breathing rhythmically in and out. Her legs began to burn, but she welcomed the feeling because as she climbed she was rewarded with greater and greater views of the surrounding mountains and valleys. At times her path would wind her through tall pine trees and aspens with their leaves quaking in the soft breeze. During those times the increasing pain in her legs and her shortness of breath was a little harder to handle, but then the trail would turn and she would break through to a vista that made it all worth it. In those moments she would just stand for a bit and let the beauty sink into her soul.

As Breeze rounded the last bend to the mountain top, her body felt exhausted in a worthwhile way, as if with each step up the mountain she had left a piece of fear or pain behind.

The view stunned her into a reverent silence. The blue of the sky, the deep green of the trees and the pure whiteness of the clouds worked together in perfect harmony to sing a lullaby to her soul. The rustling of the trees in the wind and the rushing of the mountain stream that had led her here joined the inspiring song.

Spotting a pine tree, Breeze decided to wait in its shade. The Old Man wasn't here yet but she wasn't worried. This time was different than the other times she had come to meet him. She wasn't panicking or in despair. She wasn't angry at him or fearful he wouldn't come. She knew he would come. Leaning back against the tree, she surveyed the beauty around her and waited patiently, calmly.

She laid a hand on her stomach and an involuntary smile stole across her face as she felt the life growing within. The other hand she placed on her heart. Her smile widened as she felt the new life growing there, as well.

"Good day, Breeze."

With the smile still resting on her face, she turned to him. "Old Man," she acknowledged with a slight nod of her head.

He was standing there with the relaxed, easy confidence she had come to know as one of his defining characteristics. His simple linen clothes were neat and tidy, the colors blending in with the scene around him.

"Thank you for meeting me here today," she said, her smile filling her countenance, as she thought of all the other times she had met him since her journey began and how different this meeting felt.

"I will always be here when you need me," he promised, and then chuckled as he added, "although you might not always like what I have to say."

Breeze laughed as she responded, "I'm sure of it."

"Now, why are we here?" he asked.

"Drake would like to reconcile, and I'm not sure what to do."

"That is a hefty decision to make."

"What should I do?" she asked, turning to face him.

"Well, it is not always that simple. Sometimes, how and why you make a decision, is just as important as the decision you make. Do not ignore the process of making a decision, for there is much to be gained by the journey. You can learn important things about yourself as you contemplate which path to take."

Breeze couldn't help but admit that she felt a little disappointed.

"I can't come up to the mountain again tomorrow," she countered. "Dad needs me in the shop and I need to give Drake my decision."

"I have two more gifts to give you," he said, reaching into a pocket on his tunic and pulling out a rock to hand to Breeze.

"A rock," Breeze said flatly.

She was startled when the Old Man laughed out loud. Putting his arm around her shoulders, he gave them a gentle squeeze.

"Do you remember that you looked at the key I gave you the same way?"

Breeze smiled at the memory.

"Alright, yes, I remember," she answered. "Tell me about your rock."

"First, feel it," he instructed.

Obediently, Breeze rubbed the smooth surface of the stone.

"It's very smooth, almost like glass," she reported.

"This rock became smooth by being still."

Breeze looked into the Old Man's eyes, trying to understand where this conversation was leading.

"I took this rock from a river bed," he continued. "If it had tumbled along with the current it wouldn't feel the way it does. It became smooth because it was still and let the water rush past. When you have decisions to make, whether big or small, find stillness in your mind, like the stone. Let your thoughts, emotions, and expectations rush past. Let the thoughts, emotions and expectations of others around you rush past as well. But you be still. It is in that stillness that you will find me. I may come to you as a thought or a feeling or as something you suddenly and simply know to be true, but I will come to you."

Breeze felt hope rising within her as she rubbed the smooth surface of the rock. She knew she would be able to access the wisdom and healing of the Old Man anytime and anywhere, and that gave her peace. She dropped the stone in her pocket but unlike when she first dropped the key in that same pocket, she knew she would use this gift.

"Now for the second gift I have to give you. I want to tell you your real name."

"My real name?"

"Yes. Do you want to know it?"

She wasn't sure. She had always known that Breeze wasn't her real name but it had been so long since she had heard her real name she had forgotten it. It felt odd to think of having a different name, as if it would make her a different person somehow. But wasn't she? After what she had been through she knew she would never be the same person again. She also knew that she liked the person she was becoming. So, a new name? Why not?

"'Yes, I would like to know."

"Your real name is Aspen." He paused and looked at her, waiting to see if the name had any impact. "Do you know anything about aspens?"

Puzzled, she shook her head.

"They are remarkable trees. Aspens are one of the largest living things on earth. They don't look like it above ground but underneath, where no one can see, huge groves of aspens are all connected to each other through the same roots. Aspens can heal with their bark and their leaves. The bark of an aspen can help spark a fire, even when it's wet."

The Old Man seemed pleased with this information but Breeze was still confused. Why was it so important for her to climb all the way to the top of this mountain to find out she was named after a tree? Sensing her confusion, the Old Man took her hand in his and looked steadily into her eyes.

"Aspen," he began. It sounded so strange, not like her name at all. "You are so much more than a pleasant, summer breeze which is lightly felt and easily forgotten. You are connected in unseen ways to those around you.

You heal people. You heal their bodies and with the knowledge you are gaining you will begin to help them heal their souls. You will help light fires in the hearts of those whose flames have gone out."

It seemed too big of a promise but she wanted it to be true. She wanted to share with others the peace the Old Man had helped her find.

"If I use the keys you have given me, and live the way you have taught me, can I have peace, and even be happy, no matter what happens between me and Drake?" She knew she already knew the answer, but she wanted to ask, just one more time.

The Old Man stood and, taking Aspen by the hand, pulled her to her feet. Taking both her hands in his, he looked intently at her face.

"You will go forward from this moment and write your own story. And yes, if you live the principles I have taught you, it will have a happy ending." He lifted her chin with his hand. "Remember this: it is when you find yourself, not when you find your prince, that your fairytale ending begins."

Leaning forward, the Old Man kissed her forehead. She felt the healing warmth she had grown accustomed to feeling in his presence flow through her body.

"Now, go," he said. "You have important decisions to make and lives to bless. I will see you again soon."

"Yes," agreed Aspen. "I will see you soon."

The Beginning

About the Author

Rebecca lives in the wild and wonderful hills with her three small children and one big dog. She enjoys gardening, reading, hiking, camping, and learning new things.

Printed in the United States
by Baker & Taylor Publisher Services